I0526036

also by David Bachelor:

Sweet By and By

Dorothea and Preston

a story of love

Dorothea
and
Preston

a story of love

DAVID BACHELOR

Dorothea and Preston: a story of love

Digital ISBN: 978-1-940769-02-8
Print ISBN: 978-0-9892882-9-3

Publisher: Mercury HeartLink

Albuquerque, New Mexico

Printed in the United States of America

Cover photo "Grand Haven Lighthouse", John McCormick

This is a work of fiction. Any similarity to persons living or dead is merely coincidental.

Contact the author: *dbachelor@mac.com*

Mercury HeartLink
www.heartlink.com

DORTHEA & PRESTON

Part One

MAY 1940

Part Two

AUGUST 1940

Part Three

NOVEMBER 1940

Acknowledgements

Folk wisdom tells us that it takes a village to raise a child. A child is most certainly the product of a varied and powerful environment. When an individual creates a novel, if he is honest, he will recognize that the story is the result of wide influences. By my limited and subjective assessment, this novel has required the voluntary and involuntary contributions of two families and many friends as well as a few who would not care to be included in the latter category.

Dorothea and Preston: A Story of Love is a fictional tale that grapples with fundamental life, death and moral issues. Such grappling, the success and failure of dealing with deep issues, draws on who and what I am. I have learned from others and I now feel I have something to pass on.

This is the place where I honor my teachers and attest that errors are my own.

From my mother and father I learned what honesty I have. They taught me to question everything, to recognize and examine my values.

From my siblings I have learned genuine bravery and clarity of vision.

From Luisa, her large and distinguished family I have learned kindness, love and humility.

I have been blessed too with friends who taught by example and love.

I am a fortunate and happy person. I recognize the value of what I have been taught though I may not always apply the lesson.

Part One

May 1940

Chapter 1

Out of the west, a breeze, cooled by its sweep across Lake Michigan, swirled along the streets of Lake Harbor. Waves rolled onto the beach and collapsed. Above the lake and inland, past the paved road outlining the shore, the houses of the town remained shuttered and dark. Some inhabitants rolled over and tried to stretch their sleep time, though the morning sun was chasing away the night shadows. It was Friday, May 3, 1940.

Sheer curtains, freshly washed and hung the past week, waved over the bed. Dorothea Dolan woke, groaned, and pulled the blanket over her right shoulder. She'd slept soundly, but running her boarding house for the elderly was demanding work. Her calling was to cook and clean for her charges, and she was happy with that decision.

She sat up abruptly and shook her head, tossing her short hair. Yawning hugely, she scratched her scalp. Blinking away the dryness in her eyes, she surveyed her peaceful domain. Alone in her own double bed, the large room gave her pleasure every time she saw it. She did not mind the three sets of stairs she had to climb to get to her room. The slanted ceiling of her room beneath the eaves did not bother her either. She'd learned when to duck.

Plumping the pillow, she lay back with her hands behind her head. She couldn't fall asleep again. But it was too early to get up just yet. Listening to the waves and feeling the breeze on her skin was soothing, almost better than sleep. She shook a cigarette from a pack of Lucky Strikes on the bedside table and lit it with a paper match.

From the floor below where her boarders slept in small, separate rooms, someone was coughing. Phlegmy spasms went on until Dorothea was sure the sufferer would be without breath. But the hacking ended and after a short silence a thin, wavering sound echoed upward as if someone was having a nightmare. The sounds seemed to her to have come from different people. Dorothea inhaled cigarette smoke deeply and said a silent prayer that no one was getting sick. Her guests were feeble and had not had easy lives. She loved them, and was fully aware that love involved obligations. There was so much pain and misery in the world. It broke her heart to see one of her guests suffer.

Dorothea would not allow any of them to dwell with pain very long. When she was convinced that a boarder was doomed to a long, painful decline, Dorothea would end that downward spiral quickly and with as little pain as possible. It was her final gift to her guest and she'd do her duty whether it was legal or not. She lived her life in service to the people who roomed with her.

When she was growing up there had been little time for relaxing and she had known little of love. Life had been filled with fear. The two-room shanty she had grown up in had been so close to the railroad track that ran past the Indiana hamlet that the flimsy board and batten walls shook every time a train passed.

With eight other siblings sleeping in one room there had been no chance for quiet reflection. From the other room there often came her father's angry swearing and her mother's pleas as he beat her.

If Dorothea's father made a little money as a day-laborer at one of the large farms there would be his rattling snores as he slept off the drunk. When the liquor ran out Dorothea and the kids would bear the cruel weight of his hangover. Even now Dorothea sometimes felt an ominous threat when she was surrounded by silence.

Mom. She remembered pale skin and sad eyes; how her frail mother flinched when her father came close. The only food in the house was bought with the money her mother earned washing clothes for other families.

After an especially brutal round of beatings, somber men entered the house. They went into the room where her parents slept and came out with a pitifully slender bundle wrapped in a threadbare quilt. That had been the last time she'd seen her mother.

Father disabled by alcohol, Dorothea tried to care for the other kids. She could still feel the pain in her hands as she remembered doing the wash or lifting the iron pot in which the miserable gruel that was their meal was prepared. Beyond the physical discomfort there was the pain in her heart as she listened to the littlest children's confused and desperate fears. Denny had been the youngest and had responded to the death of their mother by desperately hanging onto Dorothea.

Her mother died in 1911 when Dorothea was ten. By fourteen she knew that the unending work and abuse doomed her to sharing the same fate as her mother. The rough and increasingly urgent sexual demands of the older neighbor boys precipitated Dorothea's decision to leave. Alerting the local orphanage so that the little ones would be fed and sheltered, she left. It had been an act of desperation that had saddened her ever since.

Dorothea walked away from the shanty with only a small bundle of clothes and her resolve. She'd had no plan other than to get as far away as she could and then knock on doors asking for work. Luck had favored her when on the second day of inquiring, after a cold night spent trying to sleep in a ditch, Dorothea got a job as the live-in helper for an elderly lady, Granny Quinn. Her new employer had built up a business sewing dresses for rich matrons who came in their coaches from Indianapolis. She was old fashioned and expected a full day's work from her new maid. Dorothea did not mind hard work and long hours. Meals were regular and Dorothea got to sleep on a soft pallet by the stove in the kitchen.

Mornings she brought Granny a cup of tea and sat with her. Granny called her sweetheart, patted her hand and talked to her of the plans for the day. Dorothea would have done anything for her.

"Keep your eyes wide open, Dorothea," Granny advised her as she sipped the tea. "Keep them open and trained right on your goals."

"When you put on a little weight you'll be a pretty girl, sweetheart. There's going to be a crowd of men trying to get you to go along with them. Don't let them do it. Don't let nobody take your ambitions away."

After the tea was drunk, Dorothea helped the old lady get dressed, a slow and increasingly painful task as her rheumatism worsened. As Dorothea's skills increased she gradually took over the active work of measuring and fitting the dresses. She learned to help Granny's customers out of their dresses and into robes to be comfortable during the long fitting sessions. Dorothea adroitly handled the tape measure and learned to hold straight pins in her mouth as she fetched water or tea or the latest copy of the American magazine for the bored ladies.

Sometimes an appreciative customer would give Dorothea a coin. Sitting nearby, Granny missed nothing. When they were alone she'd waggle her finger at Dorothea and intone, "Pennies make dollars" or "Coins make paper." The young woman would carefully add the money to her slowly growing cache.

The harsh winter of 1921, when Dorothea was almost twenty, Granny Quinn became bedridden. There was little need for her to get up anymore since the dressmaking business had ceased. Ladies from the big city were not traveling in the harsh weather. Dorothea had been with Granny for about five years by then and matured into a strong, capable woman. She did not mind the weather or the lack of business. Granny's care took up her days and staying busy kept her warm.

"You be careful, sweetheart." Granny's voice quavered weakly. "Be careful of the sweet talkers." Often pain would end her advice. When the old lady's lips were pressed together so tightly they were white, Dorothea knew it was time to carefully measure out the drops of opium tincture, the bitterness masked by some mint oil. Then Granny would sleep.

On another evening when Granny felt stronger, she told Dorothea, "Sweetheart, you need to think about moving on. Me and the business are done for. You've got your whole life to live." Dorothea nodded courteously but did not want to think about life without Granny.

As the old lady's pain grew so did the frequency with which Dorothea measured out the drops of opium. Winter had almost run its course when late one night Granny summoned Dorothea.

"Sweetheart, if you love me, you'll help me. End this pain." She pointed toward the dresser where the medicine sat. Weeping,

Dorothea could not look into her tortured eyes. In her heart she knew she must help. Slowly she rose, went to the dresser and mixed the drink. Granny smiled and patted her hand. Dorothea sat through the night with her mentor.

Granny died that night. Later Dorothea learned that Granny had left her enough money for her to be independent for a while. More importantly, that night she sat with the old lady had taught Dorothea the truth about love.

In her bedroom, Dorothea checked the clock on the bedside table. She closed the window now that the lake breeze was chilly. There was time before she needed to start breakfast. It was Friday so she'd scramble eggs and sprinkle cinnamon sugar on buttered toast. It would be a treat for the people staying with her. She provided room and board for elderly folks who were alone and had a bit of income to pay the monthly charge of $15.00. She provided her roomers with breakfast and dinner every day but Sunday. Keeping the meals simple and predictable made Dorothea's work easier. The old folks knew what was on the menu every day and the predictability somehow eased their minds.

Before she started breakfast she'd check the mailbox for the early delivery. Retirement checks for those former guests who had been rescued from their pain still arrived every month. Dorothea experienced no guilt as she forged the names of the deceased. Those who had gone to their rest were helping out those who still needed her help.

Bills needed paying and even with the monthly checks her business was just breaking even. She'd have to find some new roomers. Worrying wouldn't help, she reminded herself. Everyone was having a rough time. The depression that had struck the economy a near fatal blow almost a decade ago still held business by the throat. Even the reform programs and optimistic speeches by the president, Franklin Delano Roosevelt,, had not made life much easier for the common folks.

She threw back the covers, the big-time politicians could run the country. Dorothea needed to take care of her own business. Her roomers relied on her; she'd take care of them.

Chapter 2

"Time to get up, lazybones," Dorothea voiced the order and laughed as she rolled out of the double bed. Straightening her cotton nightgown, for a moment she let the breeze press the material against her body. Gazing at her image in the cheval mirror, she judged that she looked pretty good. She was approaching forty, not that she let anybody know, but her body was still slender and fit. Leaning closer to the silvered surface she inspected her hair. There were no gray strands yet and her hazel eyes were bright. With a little reluctance she put on her robe, belted it, and put on her slippers.

Had that cry earlier this morning been from Alma? One of her roomers sometimes imagined she heard voices. The coughing probably was from Max Volstad. He had not been well. She must remember to check on both this morning.

Dorothea moved across the room to a far corner where there was a small zinc sink, a counter running the width of the room, and cabinets above. On the counter top there was a hot plate where she warmed soup on the Sundays she didn't want to leave the room. She kept her WearEver drip coffee maker next to the hot plate.

Opening a cabinet she searched among the dishes and cans for her coffee canister. Dorothea spotted the half-empty bottle of

Gordon's gin. She gazed at the clear liquid longingly. A shot would alleviate the slight headache she had this morning. Last night she was so tired her body ached. She couldn't relax. As she got ready for bed a few nips eased her discomfort but she'd drunk a bit too much.

"Nope, girl. No morning shot for you. There's a busy day ahead." She moved the bottle aside, took down the Eight O'Clock coffee canister and spooned grounds into the basket.

While the coffee brewed Dorothea went into another of her luxuries. In a small room opposite the bed was her very own washroom and toilet. The cubicle was a converted closet so it was scarcely big enough for her to stretch out her arms. Cramped it was but the space was all hers and only *her* cosmetics were lined up on the ledge beneath the mirror. She hummed as she washed vigorously in the cold water.

In the mirror above the sink she examined her face and imagined hearing Mary Fulton's loud laughter. Mary was Dorothea's best friend. Last Sunday they had seen "Gone With the Wind" at the Sun Cinema. As was their habit they'd stopped for a Coca-Cola at Flanders Drug Store to share their impressions of the film and exchange the recent gossip. She recalled how Mary's expressive face revealed her feelings as she recounted the destruction of Atlanta.

"That Scarlett," Mary announced as her dark eyes glistened, "she picked the right one, that tall guy. Fellow who played Ashley Wilkes, what was his name?"

"Leslie Howard," Dorothea responded.

"Yeah, he can put his boots under my bed anytime."

"Mary." She cautioned her friend and then giggled into her hand. When excited her friend talked loudly. Dorothea looked around and was relieved none of the other customers seemed to have heard. Mary Fulton had a husband after all.

"Who'd you favor, Dorothea?" Mary's question awoke her from her reverie. She had been remembering her life in Hollywood after Grannie Quinn died. There had been the all-too short time with Philippe.

"Dorothea?"

"Sorry. I don't like my men skinny." Dorothea spoke softly. "Now I'm not looking for a man but I sure wouldn't mind if Clark Gable showed up on my porch with some flowers." She began to laugh. "That little mustache must tickle."

Mary joined her laughter. Out of breath they sipped their Cokes through waxed straws. After several moments of reflective silence Dorothea looked up and saw that Mary was staring at her.

In response to her inquiring look Mary said, "I was thinking that you look just like Scarlett. You know, the actress, what's her name? Her hair is longer is all."

"Vivien Leigh," Mary never remembered names.

Back in her tiny washroom Dorothea held back her thick hair with a pink headband and smiled as she applied face cream. Her friend was a real card.

Mary's compliment led her to wonder if Vivien Leigh had tiny wrinkles round her eyes too. The mirror sure showed the tiny lines around her eyes and at the corners of her lips. Dorothea supposed the money she spent on anti-aging lotions might have been better spent on her business, but for her such cosmetics were necessities. In her core she knew she would be safe and strong as long as she was strong and independent, as long as she made the decisions. She refused to picture herself old, feeble, being cared for by others. What would have come of dear Grannie Quinn if Dorothea hadn't been there to help her?

She made up her eyes and then decided to wait to put on her bright red lipstick. No need to stain her coffee cup. After she'd had her coffee she'd finish her makeup. Now was her planning time, her last period of privacy before she would begin the task of caring for her charges.

On the floor below, a door slammed and someone coughed and muttered plaintively. This time she was sure it was Max Volstad, her longest boarder. The old sailor was declining rapidly and had become feeble, querulous. The toilet flushed and there was more muttering before the door to his room banged shut. Max was going to wake the entire house Dorothea thought with a touch of resentment. But the house was silent again.

She gazed at her face again. That little mustache on Clark's lip sure was cute. It had been so long since there'd been a man in her life. "That'll be enough out of you, hussy." She whispered the order to the mirror.

Leaving the toilet she returned to the big room and went to the coffee pot and poured a cup. What was on the schedule for today? There was breakfast to fix first. It was at the morning meal that she checked to make sure her guests were healthy, comfortable and clean. She instructed all her new guests that they were to keep themselves and their rooms clean. But they were old and sometimes grew careless, especially Max. Gus, her other male roomer, was slowing down too. While they ate she'd look them over to see if anyone seemed ill or especially uncomfortable. Then she'd looked in on them after breakfast to make sure beds were made, garbage taken out and that the rooms were aired.

On matters of personal hygiene she had to be especially careful with Max. Age and physical disabilities caused him to wait too long between baths. She needed to make her suggestions gentle and indirect. The old sailor was proud and imagined he was still fit and strong.

And then there was Alma. She was the youngest of her current guests, barely into her sixties. But Alma sometimes heard voices. The voices confused her, urging her to do self-destructive things like drink too much alcohol, and bring men to her room. Last night Dorothea thought she'd heard Alma stumble when she came in. Perhaps the voices were pestering the poor thing again. There'd been the groaning and cries. She'd have to keep an eye on Alma at breakfast.

After the meal she'd go to Finnegan's Farmer's Market. Mrs. Meacham, one of her neighbors, had told her over the back fence yesterday evening that the Market had a sale on early peas and potatoes. Then she might stop in at Meraggio's Butcher Shop to see if there were some good deals.

She liked to feed her guests well, but meat was so expensive: bacon was up to $0.50 a pound. Sometimes Sal Meraggio would sell her hamburger at $0.40 a pound, a few cents off the regular price. The savings tempted Dorothea but Sal was smitten with her and tried to create opportunities to get her in his back room and touch her. The butcher was another man who needed careful treatment.

Fridays were especially busy since after shopping there was her card party with the girls in the evening. She didn't mind the extra work, the hurrying. It was her chance to meet with Mary and other friends; playing cards was just an excuse to get together, have a few drinks and gossip.

Cup empty, she set it in the sink. It was time to care for her charges.

Chapter 3

"Breakfast is ready. Come get it while it's hot," Dorothea called up the rear stairs. She picked up the bowl of hot scrambled eggs and hurried from the kitchen through the double sliding doors to the dining room.

The table was set. In the middle of the long wooden table, covered by the green quilted warmer embroidered with roses, were the slices of toast she prepared earlier. Next to the toast was a large ceramic pitcher of strong coffee. At each of the four places she portioned out eggs onto the plates. Behind her there were the sounds of rushing steps on the stairs: Alma's quick, light pace followed by the heavy uneven clump of Max and his cane.

Alma entered the dining room and scurried to her usual seat. "Oh, dear Dorothea, thank you so much. I am so hungry, absolutely famished," Alma gushed as she pulled out her chair, sat down and snatched a slice of warm, buttered toast from the warmer.

She chewed steadily, swallowed and filled her mouth with eggs. Beneath her uneven halo of gray hair Alma smiled benignly around the room.

"Is that a new dress, dear?" Dorothea asked as she filled Alma's mug with coffee. "Peach favors your coloring."

Alma's smile widened. "I found this on the rack at the

church resale shop. It was a little expensive. But I just had to have it. I'm so glad you like it."

One of Dorothea's main concerns had already been settled this morning. Alma's bright eyes and vivacious manner meant that the voices weren't torturing her. When she was afflicted she was quiet, distant and her appetite failed.

Max limped into the room leaning heavily on his cane. He coughed, grumbling wordlessly, and sat heavily in his regular chair at the end of the table.

A chino shirt, vest and dungarees made up his daily uniform. She poured coffee into his mug, sniffed and made a mental note to start campaigning to get Max to take a bath.

"Where's Gus? Is he sick?" she asked. Gus Brewer, a semi-retired carpenter, roomed next to Max and sat by him at meals.

Alma shrugged, too disinterested to stop chewing. Her lack of interest in men was another sign of the remission of her mental problems. Max looked up, bits of egg caught up in his full mustache, and growled one word, "Whiskey."

Dorothea was disappointed. Gus seemed to be a stable, dependable fellow. She hoped he wasn't going to take to hiding in his room drinking. In the past, a few of her boarders had used alcohol to try to escape their problems.

Dorothea kept her own drinking under strict control. Her guests, Max particularly, drank whiskey regularly. Alma, when she was afflicted, drank in the taverns that dotted the streets leading west down to the docks.

Though Dorothea felt her rooming house ought to be genteel she tried to be understanding and tolerant. Her guests were not wealthy and had lived difficult lives, had worked hard at sometimes dangerous jobs. Now old and infirm, unable to afford proper medical care, they often used alcohol as a cheap, readily available painkiller.

Max raised his head and nodding to emphasize his words, offered an explanation. "Him and Louise," he named Gus's lady friend, "had a falling out sure enough. Gus tell me." He intoned, "women be nothing but trouble." The old man added as he looked at Dorothea, "Not to worry, he be down for his eats still. Moving slow he is. Got a sore head I bet."

As if on cue there were the sounds of hurrying feet on the stairs and a tall, skinny man his lank black hair reaching almost to his shoulders, and dressed in threadbare work clothes hurried to the remaining place. After a muttered apology he sat down and slowly ate his breakfast. Every once in a while he would sigh and run his large, calloused hand over his forehead and through his hair.

The room's silence was broken by the sounds of eating and the soft requests for condiments or toast. Dorothea got up and brought out the skillet, offering the remaining scrambled eggs. Gus didn't want any more so Alma and Max split what was left. Finished with her meal, Dorothea refilled coffee cups and sat down to rest a bit before washing the dishes.

"Dorothea," Alma asked, "did you have your radio on last night at about 8 0'clock?"

"No, Alma," she smiled at the tiny, expectant face, "I had some things to wash out and then went to bed."

"You work too hard, poor dear. The Jimmy Dorsey Band performed. I love to hear him play the clarinet. They played "The Things I Love." She hummed the tune of the love song and sang some lines in a quavering soprano: "The golden flicker of the fireflies, the gleam of love light in your lovely eyes."

Alma sighed and smiled at Dorothea. "The show came all the way from New York City, some hotel, a fancy one I bet."

Her soft voice was drowned out by a loud, long, slowly fading whoop. After the whistle was silent the cacophonous squawks of distant gulls drifted into the room.

"That be City of Milwaukee coming to Grand Trunk railroad dock," Max muttered as he munched the last piece of toast.

"Oh, I just love the sound of those boats. So romantic." Alma enthused.

Max grumped, "Ships, they be ships, woman. You think it is romantic working on a train ferry? You be out on the Lake, waves over the ship, damned railroad cars maybe slipping around on deck. You get wet and wind freeze you to death." For confirmation he nodded at Gus. But the dark-haired man was staring into his half empty cup as if searching for an answer to a vexing question.

Alma beamed at the old man. "Dangerous to be sure, but exciting. Am I correct, Mr. Volstad?"

"Yeah, sure," his deep voice was sarcastic. "Pretty exciting to drown. Old Milwaukee train ferry went down six, seven years ago. Fifty-two men drowned; friends some of them." The last part of Max's career as a sailor had been spent working on the train ferries that carried loaded railroad cars from Milwaukee, Wisconsin to the Grand Trunk Railroad tracks at Lake Harbor, Michigan to avoid the long and expensive trip around the southern tip of Lake Michigan through Chicago.

"I am sure there was danger, Mr. Volstad." Alma gave up on the old sailor and switched her smile to Dorothea. "The Dorsey band was very nice. Next week the program is featuring Mr. Bing

Crosby."

Dorothea smiled back. She loved to listen to music while she rested. But lately for Dorothea just listening was not enough. What a thrill it would be to dance in a New York City hotel wearing a pretty lace gown. Philippe had taken her dancing and he'd had a mustache. She grew a little dizzy at the memory. Clark Gable probably held his dance partners so close that they could feel each other's warmth. Gown material was so thin.

"War. Do you think there'll be war in Europe, Dorothea? The news I hear on the radio everybody's threatening everybody, troops always marching here and there. Mr. Roosevelt in his last fireside chat said there might be." Alma looked around bright eyes blinking.

Why couldn't people learn to get along, Dorothea thought? "Alma, I don't know." She hated to be so terse with Alma but time was rushing by and she needed to wash the dishes and get going on her busy day.

She tried to end the conversation gently. "Dear, it is hard enough just getting by these days."

"You damn right," Max growled disregarding Dorothea's scowl at his use of language. The old man winced as he moved his foot to a more comfortable position. "Roosevelt's a Bolshevik. Get us in a war sure enough. New Deal, bah. Hitler and that Italian guy, they know how to get things sorted out, sure enough. Get all the trains running on time, sure enough."

Finished speaking, he thumped his empty coffee mug down on the table and struggled to stand up. The noise roused Gus from his reverie. His eyes were moist. He said nothing as he slowly rose.

Alma smiled at Dorothea, wrinkles hiding her eyes, jumped

up and ran around Gus to get to the stairs first. Her shoes made a staccato racket as she ran up to her room. Dorothea, laden with utensils and dishes, went to the kitchen. Max slowly limped toward the stairs followed by Gus.

The empty room was filled again with the warning whistle from the ship on the lake. The shriek was answered by the urgent cries of the gulls.

Chapter 4

When Preston Duhamel awoke it was always the same: a sudden flinch, a rush of fear followed by the listening for the chatter of machine guns. When he was fully awake there was a surge of guilt. All those fellows falling and he could do nothing. The fear dissipated. From the trees outside his window chirping of newly roused sparrows reminded him that he was a patient in the City Hospital in New York City. It was May 3, 1940 and Preston was being treated for chronic alcoholism.

He got up slowly as his room filled with sunlight coming through the cloudless sky. The high narrow bed carefully made, he gathered his toiletries in the leather zipper case resting on the small chest of drawers. Preston slowly opened the door to the hallway. The hinges creaked and he did not want to disturb the other patients. Some of them were in really bad shape.

Limping, he made his way down the hallway to the communal men's room. The shadowed passage reminded Preston of Killer Kane. That homicidal thief had put a bullet in his hip and now he would always walk in a slightly lopsided fashion.

Before the gun battle he'd been drunk for a week, but covered his condition well. Despite his addiction to alcohol he was a successful detective. He had been appointed to head a five-member flying squad to chase down Killer Kane and his two henchmen. Preston's squad cornered the gang in a roadhouse outside a hamlet in northern Michigan. In the following firefight, in a fit of drunken bravado, Preston chased down Kane and killed him. The successful outcome had not come cheaply. The Kane gang was wiped out, while Preston's squad suffered two wounded and one killed.

A reporter for a national wire service wrote about the incident and called Preston "a warrior-hero." A spate of articles described his service in World War I as well as his career as a cop. Preston learned that journalism of that time did not always involve a great deal of truthfulness.

The newspaper attention had saved his job. His superiors in the State Police Department had been ready to fire him for his drunkenness but feared the negative publicity and public reaction were the "Hero" to be punished. The wealthy owner of the string of newspapers paid for Preston's well-publicized recovery from the hip wound as well as a quiet period of recovery from alcoholism in City Hospital.

Preston washed his face, shaved, brushed his teeth and washed again. Deep in his heart was the fear that though he had not had a drink for four weeks, he would be fired nevertheless. Newspaper attention had moved on to a Hollywood sex scandal so Preston was no longer protected.

After combing his straight black hair, he noticed a slight change in the color of his sideburns. Leaning closer to the mirror he located some gray strands. "Ah, time marches on, my boy," he murmured, smoothing back his hair. Leaning a bit closer he inspected his bloodshot blue eyes. Almost as bad as when he was drinking, he judged. Now the redness and burning in his eyes was from insomnia. Sleep did not come easily most nights even with the medicine given him as part of the belladonna treatment. When he dozed the nightmares tortured him. He sighed and gathered up his kit and walked slowly down the shadowed hallway back to his room.

Preston closed the door behind him and sat heavily on the straight-back chair, moist towel draped over his shoulder. Soon there would be the hurried squeak of the nurses' shoes as they tapped on each door. Most drunks did not want to get up, preferred to sleep late but the hospital regimen required all patients to be up early to begin the day's activity. Soon Nurse Rachel, a pretty lass, a shame she was so serious, would tap on his door. First there would be a light breakfast in the first floor dining hall, then the day's pills and exercises.

He'd better get a shirt on. From the narrow closet next to the head of his high, narrow bed he took his last clean short-sleeve sports shirt off the hanger and buttoned it up. It was a weekday so he'd be able to do a wash tonight when the hospital routine was done. There was a tremor in his hands as he slipped the buttons into the holes. The nervousness rose from worry about the decisions about his future. He'd been here almost two weeks and the normal program was one week. Had the State Police authorities forgotten him?

Dressed, he was ready for the tap on the door. The sparsely furnished room reflected the way he felt inside this morning. It was a barracks more than a hospital. Preston had spent most of his adult life alone in places like this. First it had been the Marines then the Michigan State Police. The two and a half years he'd been married to Edith was the only period he hadn't lived in spartan conditions with other men.

The good part of his marriage, the passion and the birth of his daughter Solange, had not lasted long. Edith soon told him that the life of a cop's wife did not suit her. Preston had loved being a trooper. Riding the red Indian motorcycle, racing along the highway chasing law-breakers was a thrilling way to serve society. For a short time her sharp words softened. At her behest he'd passed the exam and became a detective. He gave up the motorcycle for a desk and dressed like a clerk. He'd bought a little bungalow in Ann Arbor. But soon afterward the marriage collapsed beneath the weight of his drinking and the other women.

Edith had thrown him out. Later he'd heard that she married a dentist and moved to New Hampshire. Preston sent little gifts to his daughter on her birthday and Christmas. In return he received printed "Thank You" cards carefully signed by Solange.

"Come in," Preston said in response to the tap on his door.

The door opened and a slight, pretty young woman stood at the threshold. She frowned, avoiding his eyes as she looked across the room and out the window.

Preston suppressed the smile that pulled at his face. When he saw Nurse Rachel he always thought of Pygmalion. The unsmiling nurse needed the attentions of a caring and experienced older man. A quiet summer afternoon spent with the young woman in the stiffly starched uniform would do them both a world of good.

"Yes," he said and rose.

"Please wait here. Walt will be up to see you before breakfast."

Preston sat down again.

☙   ☙   ☙

In a few minutes there was a loud thump on the door and it swung open to reveal the short stature of Walt, the man Preston had been talking to since he arrived at the hospital. Before alcohol had crushed him and driven his family away Walt had been a successful salesman. He could, he told Preston, sell refrigerators to Eskimos. Standing as straight as a drill sergeant on parade grounds, he entered the room, chest stuck out.

"Morning, Preston, you okay?" At Preston's nod, Walt drew a business-size envelope from his jacket pocket and held it out. Walt did not smile and waited patiently as Preston took it, tore off the flap and read the contents.

After reading the sentences on the page twice, Preston handed the missive to Walt. He nodded abruptly, cleared his throat and read aloud the single typewritten sheet:

```
From the Office of Inspector Myron Finley
Chief Michigan State Police Detective Division
To Detective Preston Duhamel

You are hereby directed to report to the State
Police Barracks at East Lansing, Michigan,
there to reside until you receive further
directions from Inspector Finley.
```

Below the inspector's scribbled signature there were instructions concerning bus schedules and the securing of vouchers to pay his fare.

"Well," Walt spoke loudly, his voice deep from inside his chest. "Well, Preston, you've been sprung. Smile, you are going home."

Preston did not know how to answer his counselor. Home? He smiled wanly and tried to remember when he did have a home.

"Here, my friend," Walt intoned holding out his hand. "Let me shake your hand. I've seen your progress here. Told Mister Townes, the hospital administrator, I'd bet all I had that you were cured of your obsession with the bottle. He told that to your boss in Michigan. Now they want you back. I know when someone is cured of their desire to drink."

"Thanks for your confidence Walt but ..." Preston's head felt muddled and confused. There was something he should tell Walt but he wasn't sure what it was.

"My boy, don't be modest. You and I have worked hard on your problem. You are cured." Walt looked closely at his patient. "Seen hundreds of men leave here and all of them were nervous, anxious. Not to worry, my boy. You are a Marine. I've seen your military record. Wounded at Belleau Woods in 1918. A Purple Heart and a Bronze Star. Those medals aren't handed out to just anybody. You are a brave man, well trained. You have learned discipline. You will do well." Walt pulled out his handkerchief and blew his nose loudly. "Anything you want to say, my boy?

Preston did not want to hear anymore pep talk garnished with his biography so he looked away and shook his head.

Walt shook his hand vigorously and then left the room.

Chapter 5

The laughter ringing in Barracks One of the Michigan State Police Headquarters in East Lansing, Michigan ended abruptly. A young trooper, half dressed in his blue uniform, looked at the wooden floor as he flushed deeply. Preston got up from his narrow bunk clad in a threadbare tee shirt and shorts. The ragged clothes did not diminish the decisiveness in his voice and bearing. He stepped in front of the trooper and repeated his question, "I asked you, Trooper Nolan, what did you call me?"

"I called you Frenchie, Detective Duhamel sir." The tall officer drew himself up straight and looked at his superior squarely. "I meant no disrespect."

Preston returned the level look. "You are correct. I am of French descent. My family moved from eastern Canada and ended up in Michigan almost 40 years ago. I find the designation 'Frenchie' to be demeaning. I prefer the use of my given name."

"Understood, Detective Duhamel, sir."

Preston nodded and said, "My given name in these barracks, Trooper."

"Understood, Preston, sir."

Preston took the younger man's hand and the tension in the

room relaxed. The older detective sat on his thin mattress and lit a cigarette. The young trooper continued dressing for his day. He watched the young troopers, full of energy and purpose and remembered he had nowhere to go. He had been in the barracks for a week waiting to hear from the director of the detective division. Someone yelled for help finding his boots while another needed an iron to press his wrinkled trousers.

"Hey, Ted, you doing traffic patrol?" a stocky trooper called across the wooden room addressing a blonde fellow trying to adjust his Sam Brown belt.

"Yeah," Ted replied dejectedly. "Sims and me will be cruising M66. Pray for us," he ended with a laugh of nervous bravado referring to the notorious highway running north and south in the middle of the state.

"Oh, you'll be driving the Michigan Indianapolis," Ted's stocky friend said.

"Keep those speeders from getting out of hand," advised another officer.

"Maybe stop the governor, write him a ticket," Preston said. The laughter was general. The governor's habit of rushing about the state was widely known.

"Hey, Preston, would that make him a lieutenant? Having something on the governor?"

Before Preston could reply another trooper shouted, "Lieutenant in charge of mowing the parade grounds."

The general merriment dwindled away as the men rushed to get ready to line up for roll call in the five-acre parade ground outside the barracks front door. Someone shouted, "Time." There was a general stampede out the door.

Preston stubbed out his smoke and looked about the quiet room. Ten cots were lined up on each side of a narrow central aisle. Lockers for clothes and personal items were situated at the head of each bed. Walls were painted lumber, unadorned since pictures and personal mementos were prohibited. He smiled remembering the laughing, excited young men. This was their last day on duty. When their duty ended this evening, they could go home while another barracks of troopers protected the public. He'd been a trooper before his promotion. Right after he'd been "demobbed" from the Marines in 1919 he joined the State Police.

He gathered his toiletries and went into the shower room at one end of the barracks. In the shower the warm water felt good and even cooled him off a little. But when he toweled off he could feel the beads of sweat popping out on his back. His stomach gurgled and growled though he'd not eaten very much at breakfast in the mess hall. Clad only in worn boxer shorts he stretched out on his bunk. He had a novel, a best seller about life in a valley in Wales. The story was engrossing but he had no interest in the book now. He felt no interest in doing anything. He was just an aging cop who was in trouble. Maybe his boss had decided that the force no longer needed him. What would he do if his badge was taken away?

The squeaking of the overhead fan bothered him. It was a waste of electricity since the blades did not cool off the room. In the shower room, big bluebottle flies buzzed about the puddles of water. A drink would make things better; a cool beer would ease his worry and let him relax.

He sighed and pushed the thought out of his head as Walt taught him to do. "This too shall pass." "Let go and relax." Walt had explained to him that if he'd repeat these mantras, fill his mind with the sayings, the compulsion to drink would fade. If only Walt were here to talk. If only there was somebody to talk to.

Well, there wasn't, he disciplined himself. So stop whining, Walt had warned him that obsessing about liquor could lead him back to the bottle. Alcohol was not a refuge, a hideout from the world. Face up to things, he remembered Walt's orders. He took a deep breath, closed his eyes and tried to visualize a gentle, relaxing scene.

The breeze whispered through the pines and he heard the lake waves meet the silver beach. He could feel his body relax as he recalled the sounds outside the family cabin..

BAM!

From the nearby motor pool a mechanic swung a hammer against an engine block. BAM! The percussive sound rang out again. Preston had dozed off when the clamor shocked him. He flinched and the sudden movement spasmed into a cramp in his scarred hip. Preston gritted his teeth as the barely healed muscles locked into a rock-like mass. Immobile Preston lay still and tried to will his body to relax. The pain slowly subsided and he sat up to rub his thigh and hip.

He smiled in a self-mocking way. He owed his present job to Killer Kane's bullet and the ambitious reporter at the Manchester Enterprise. Without the florid article that proclaimed Preston to be the "Fighting Marine and Hero Cop" Preston felt that he surely would have been fired. He had been warned about being drunk on duty. He'd been unable to stop drinking.

Don't get stuck in the past, he'd been advised by Walt. Face the future with optimism.

The telephone on the wall by the door rang.

Chapter 6

Dorothea stood in the shop and patiently waited for the butcher, Sal Meraggio, to finish up with Henrietta Meyer, the local minister's wife. He was a short, square-built swarthy man with broad shoulders and an expanding waistline. Coming from the backroom he moved sideways through the hallway into the shop.

"Be right with you, Miss Dolan."

"That will be fine, Mr. Meraggio." Dorothea smiled at the butcher.

Sal breathed loudly and smiled broadly at Dorothea. Laden with four dead and plucked chickens their flaccid necks pinched between his stubby fingers, Sal held the fowls up for the viewing of a worried-looking, impatient blonde.

"Mrs. Meyer, these nice fat chickens, capons, you sure like them," he announced in his fluting tenor voice as he flopped the carcasses onto a butcher block next to the glassed-in refrigerated display case. Smiling alternately at the chickens and at Mrs. Meyer he waited patiently.

Dorothea knew Henrietta Meyer. Though Dorothea had counted Henrietta as a friendly acquaintance, she surmised that she was a prominent part of Henrietta's nervousness. The minister's wife feared that one of her husband's congregation would see her and Dorothea together in the butcher shop.

"Pastor Myron Meyer's wife caught consorting with a woman of questionable morals, a keeper of a rooming house." Dorothea imagined how the headlines of the parish newspaper might read. Running a rooming house was one of the few businesses that a woman might own and operate successfully. Popular opinion held that such an occupation was immoral. Henrietta Meyers glanced behind her at Dorothea again. This time she bobbed her head in a nervous greeting. Dorothea remembered the times she helped Henrietta shovel the sidewalk in front of the Meyer house or the times she'd helped Henrietta carry home a heavy sack of groceries and grew angry.

"Henrietta how are you? Good to see you. How is Myron?" Dorothea almost shouted her greetings. The plump blonde flinched, and her heavy neck grew red as wattles. Dorothea knew she was adding to Henrietta's discomfort, but she was angry. She considered stepping closer and hugging the blonde but decided that would be too much.

Poor Sal hadn't an inkling of the dramas unfolding in his shop. He stepped closer to Henrietta and held out the carcasses, smiling broadly. Still reddened about the neck she tentatively poked one of the chickens.

"You picked the best," Sal announced enthusiastically, sounding like a radio game show host. He set the losers on the big wooden chopping block and tore a length of gleaming white paper to wrap the chicken.

While the butcher wrapped the meat Dorothea stared at the unbending back of her acquaintance. Henrietta's coat was worn, the cuffs tattered. Dorothea relaxed. Poor thing, she was so fearful.

She'd take pity on her, though were she ever to meet Henrietta Meyers in the company of one of her husband's congregants she might give her a big hug, and a kiss, too.

Clutching her purchase, the minister's wife fled the shop. Sal looked at Dorothea with a shy look that was also full of longing. His smile was an invitation to intimacy. She looked away and out the shop window onto North Fifth Street. It was a clear, sun-drenched day. Colors seemed brighter than usual as the wind off the lake snapped the flag in front of the town hall. Commerce on the main street was heavy. A wagon pulled by a skinny horse crunched over the cobblestone street. A bright yellow taxi rushed past the wagon. That driver must be doing thirty miles an hour, Dorothea estimated; he'd better be careful.

From the open door of the restaurant next door the late coffee drinkers shouted greetings to the passing crowd. "Hey, buddy," a man on his way to work waved at the owner standing at the open door, "don't take no wooden nickels."

Dorothea shifted the cloth handles of her grocery bags. The bags were heavy the handles hurt her hands. Farmers Market had had turnips and white potatoes at sale prices and she'd bought as many as she could carry. Perhaps she'd gotten too many. But she didn't have very far to go and she was strong. She set the bags down. Sal laboriously rose from placing the remaining chickens in the refrigerated display case. He came around the case and stood in front of Dorothea. She stepped backward, intimidated by the size and latent strength of the butcher. He was so close that the front of her gaily-flowered print dress was almost touched by his blood spotted butcher apron.

He looked at her slowly from her worn pumps to the bright yellow scarf tied round her hair. "Miss Dolan, you brighten the morning. Are you well?"

"Well, thank you Mr. Meraggio, what a charming thing to say. I'm fine. It's a beautiful morning isn't it?" She moved to the display case to survey the offerings. "The pork chops look good. The price tag has fallen over, how much are they?"

He hurried behind the case, sliding open the door, and retrieved the price tag. Looking at it he made a dismissive noise, showed it to Dorothea, and shook his head. "These premium chops, thick, I almost give them away. I want to help out my friends and neighbors."

She listened closely and concentrated on not smiling at the butcher's self-portrayal as a philanthropist. He went on, "These thirty-five cents a pound. But I can be your good friend, Miss Dolan. In back, I cut some for you special, thirty cents a pound. You come watch."

The price tempted Dorothea but she thought it best to fend off the invitation. "Thank you, Mr. Meraggio, the ones in the case will do very nicely. I'll take five pounds."

She'd dice the chops and with the vegetables she was carrying and the carrots in her pantry she would make a stew. It would be a healthy evening repast and she could make the food last through several meals. Boiled, the chop bones would make a tasty broth as well. Shrugging his massive shoulders Sal vacated the role of hopeful suitor and returned to that of merchant; he rushed to fill her order. As he wrapped the meat in crackling white paper the entrance bell sounded again. Dorothea turned to deposit the pork chops in her shopping bag and greeted Mildred Nowicki who had just entered the shop.

"Dorothea," Mildred responded, "how wonderful to see you.

I keep forgetting you're an early bird like me. I like to get my chores done in the morning when the weather's nice." Her gloved hand smoothed her skirt across her flat stomach. "I'm getting Stanley's supper fixed early. He has such a delicate digestion I have to be careful. Poor dear works too hard." Stanley owned a large prosperous shoe store in downtown Lake Harbor.

"I am sure he does," Dorothea said.

"Such long hours. People think that just because he owns the shoe store the money just rolls in." Mildred laughed derisively as she brushed some lint from her jacket. "They should work so hard." She inhaled prettily and adjusted her jacket. "All these government handouts, Social Security, indeed. That madman Roosevelt takes our money to give it to the moochers. Times are tough I'll tell you."

"Yes, Mildred, they are indeed." Dorothea bent over to pick up her bags. She and Mildred would see each other this evening at the regular Friday night ladies card party. Mildred was a lot of fun when she relaxed and had a drink or two but now Dorothea did not want to hear again about her skills as a housewife and how well she took care of her pudgy, balding husband.

Just out of earshot Sal waited patiently while the women talked. Dorothea appreciated his patient diplomacy. He knew well that courtesy and patience brought return business. And while they talked he could ogle Mildred Nowicki's outstanding figure. This morning she wore a very fetching gray cotton skirt just tight enough to outline her thighs. The yellow bolero jacket displayed her prominent bosom handsomely.

"Florence may not attend our next card game," Mildred announced.

Dorothea straightened up and faced her friend. "Is she

sick?"

Mildred looked about the shop enjoying the attention shown her snippet of gossip. "Yes, she's in pain, poor dear. She fell, hurt her leg."

Mildred pronounced the word "fell" with an emphasis to indicate that it was a fabrication.

Dorothea bit her lip. She must not vent her anger now in front of Meraggio and Mildred. She liked Florence Gunderson a lot. She was a big, friendly, kindly woman. But Florence Gunderson had had the damaging misfortune to marry an abusive brute. Otto Gunderson worked irregularly, and went on destructive sprees fueled by cheap booze that regularly reduced the inside of their home to splinters and their three children to fearful hysteria.

During his drunken tantrums Otto beat his gentle wife. A desperately proud woman she tried to camouflage the beatings as "accidents." Such explanations were rarely convincing though her real friends joined her in the deceit. Dorothea's rage at the man's drunken cruelty dwelt just below her civilized exterior. Memories of the cold room in Indiana and solemn men carrying her mother's bruised corpse made the murder of Otto Gunderson a possibility. Mildred noticed the butcher's attention so turned away as she secured a stray lock of honey colored hair beneath her pert hat.

"We're meeting at Mona's so we'll get to see her new furniture." Mildred turned back to whisper to Dorothea. "That Mona sure likes to show off."

She turned to the still attentive butcher. "Some nice t-bones I think. Four, please."

Dorothea picked up her bags, nodded at the butcher and her friend. Sal hurried to open the door.

She didn't notice his courtesy. Florence needed help and Dorothea was not sure what to do. She'd have to consider tactics again when she wasn't so angry.

Chapter 7

Though Preston was perspiring from the walk across the grassy parade grounds from the barracks to the director's office, he donned his jacket before he stepped to the desk and introduced himself to the receptionist. She continued to clatter at her big black Royal typewriter for several moments before turning to him.

"Detective Preston Duhamel," she pronounced his name carefully and then looked at her wristwatch. Preston recognized the move as intimidation; he was several minutes early for his 3:15 appointment. She leaned away from her typewriter and pushed a button on the intercom on her desk.

"Director Finley, Your 3:15 appointment is here. Detective Duhamel." An electronic voice crackled and grouched. "Busy now, Leona. Have him wait." Her right hand rose and the forefinger pointed at the wooden straight back chairs lined up against the wall. Obediently Preston took a seat.

A short time later, just as Leona resumed her typing, a gruff voice yelled from the office behind her, "Leona, get me those O'Brien letters."

Startled the young woman flushed as she touched the black intercom box. She shook her head, muttered something and extracted a file folder from the cabinet. She took it into the office.

As she returned to her desk Preston was able to see that his boss certainly knew how to pick good-looking help. Leona was wearing a black skirt and a white blouse with a round collar. To Preston the nun-like appearance of her outfit, and the business-like short bob of her dark blonde hair contrasted intriguingly with the cling of the skirt material to her shapely body. Looking down at her desk as she sat down, she smiled to herself. Preston turned his gaze away hurriedly when she glanced in his direction. Soon the big typewriter was rattling again.

The waiting tried his patience. When Leona stopped working to light a cigarette, Preston found he craved a smoke as well. She inhaled deeply and blew out a cloud of smoke. Another puff and she place the Lucky Strike in the ashtray as she went back to work. The smoke curled slowly upwards. At the hospital he and Walt had talked about their habits. Walt smoked too but had warned Preston not to let smoking control him. "Never allow cigarettes or booze to rule you. Strengthen your willpower." His sponsor's advice came back to him and Preston decided not to ask if he might smoke. He would take care of his business with Director Finley and then have a smoke outside. It would be a celebration cigarette or maybe a consolation one.

"Tell him to come in," the unseen director bellowed from his office. Leona smiled to herself again and shook her head. Preston was on his feet and headed to the office before she looked at him.

Director Finley held a document in his pudgy hands and read it, moving his lips slowly. He made an officious note on the page and added it to his Out-Box. He lifted his gaze to Preston. The detective stood at attention; the director did not offer his hand. The Director was a short, overweight man who preferred to sit behind his large wooden desk. Finley wore thick glasses with heavy dark frames. The round lenses and his bald head gave him the appearance of an owl, a shining, shrewd owl.

"Ah, Dremel," he said, adjusting the alignment of his pen on the blotter, centered a manila folder in front of him and opening it slowly. He licked his thin lips and held up a newspaper article.. "So you're the fella who snuffed out Killer Kane's candle." He looked at Preston for a moment and mouthed the word "Hero." Finley smiled as he put down the article and reviewed a sheaf of papers adorned with the letterhead of City Hospital.

What had they written about him? Had those doctors written that he was hopeless and worthless? Did they say that the Michigan State Police was better off without him? His back itched as beads of perspiration slowly formed and slid downwards.

The director shifted in his chair with a grunt. Finley glanced at Preston as he reached out and grabbed another stack of papers. "You all right?" The question had no warmth in it. Preston responded with a quick nod. He lifted his gaze over Finley's shining scalp to the large window behind the desk. He could see the motor pool. He had liked working on his Indian motorcycle and he'd kept it in tip-top shape. Somehow working on motors was simple. When the engine did not run, you worked on it, fixed it. Simple.

He recalled wearing his billed cap and the dark blue uniform with brass buttons and the polished Sam Browne belt. The feeling of wind rushing past his goggles as he responded to a call for help. It was a thrill atop the red Indian Chief hurrying to provide assistance. Then he'd felt fulfilled. And now he stood at attention in front of this desk sweating like a guilty schoolboy.

"Leona," the director's bellow brought Preston out of his reverie. The drum of the typewriter in the other room ceased. The director slid Duhamel's file to the side of the desk dismissively. "The Lake Harbor file." He yelled the order as if she were in the next county.

After a long silence, face averted, the secretary entered the office holding a thick manila folder. She aimed a long glance at the black intercom box on the corner of her boss' desk. Leona then placed the folder on the corner of the desk and strode out of the room. Finley grunted as he leaned over the desk and picked up the file.

He flipped it open and read slowly. He motioned for Preston to sit. The detective sat on the edge of a wooden straight back chair. "Got a job for you, Dremel. Up for it?" Finley adjusted his glasses and waited for the reply.

Preston's heart leaped when he comprehended the question. He still had a job; he was still a cop. But how the hell was he to answer the question? If he did a jig the Director might change his mind. He smiled and hoped that Finley did not see the nervous tremors running through his body. He nodded to make sure his decision was clear.

Finley slid a typed sheet of paper across the desk and motioned that Preston should read it:

On August 18, 1933, a black Buick four-door sedan stopped in front of the Peoples Savings Bank of Lake Harbor, Michigan.

Six white men wearing suits and overcoats got out of the vehicle and went in. They disarmed the guard, held guns on the tellers and customers, and made off with $14,000.

When Preston was through reading he looked up into the round face of Finley. The director smiled and said, "You were on the force then?"

Preston did not sneer though he felt the expression forming. In 1933 he'd been on the force for almost fifteen years. Where had Finley been then, still an aide to some politician? He did not shout that he had been a cop his whole life. He kept the bitterness from showing and merely nodded.

Finley turned to look out the window and spoke in a reminiscent tone. "We caught them all. The hoodlums not in jail for the rest of their lives are in the ground. We buried them." The Director's jowls wobbled dramatically. "Remember? Baby Face Nelson was in that gang of thieves in Lake Harbor. His first bank heist. He was a bad apple, loved to kill police officers. Nelson died in a ditch less than eighteen months after the Lake Harbor robbery. FBI agents shot him down. Good riddance."

And Nelson killed two FBI agents in that gun battle near Chicago. Preston silently completed the story.

"We taught those hoodlums a lesson they won't forget." Smiling, Finley leaned back in his chair until the spring mechanism protested. He cleared his throat and waved the folder. "One of the Lake Harbor bank robbers is named Theodore Bentz, alias Craig. We caught him and he's serving a life sentence in Marquette State Prison. For seven years he's been whining that his conviction was a miscarriage of justice. Claims he's never been in Lake Harbor. Says he's an innocent victim of mistaken identity and over-eager cops."

"Sir," Preston interrupted, "I recall hearing about Bentz and the allegations. I thought it had been sorted out."

Finley peered over his glasses at his underling. "Yeah, well, you're wrong. Bentz has a new lawyer. Where does the money to pay these ambulance chasers come from? Anyway, the shyster has some yellow newspapers interested. The publicity caught the attention of Hoover, the FBI director.

Finley opened a box on his desk and took out a plump cigar and lit it slowly. As he exhaled clouds of fragrant smoke he continued. "J. Edgar wants this Bentz thing checked out once and for all. We need to keep the Feds happy, so I'm sending you to Lake Harbor." He twirled the cigar in his mouth and watched the glowing end. "Make sure you talk to everybody, all the witnesses." His small hand slapped the top of the desk. "Verify everything. Show Bentz's picture around, get positive identifications. Talk to everyone involved. Do a complete job, understand?"

Finley took a 3x5 photo from the file and tossed it onto the desk. Preston picked it up. The image was of a stout, tall man wearing a three-piece suit and a fedora jauntily pushed back from his forehead. He was smiling and smoking a cigar as he leaned against the front fender of a Ford. The detective slipped the photo into his jacket pocket.

"Yes, sir."

"Take your time. Make sure Bentz stays where he belongs." He pounded the desk again. "Valuable time has been wasted on this foolishness."

"Yes, sir."

"Leona will get you a travel voucher. Get started Monday. You'll have the weekend to get yourself shipshape. Stop in Grand Rapids; the detective in charge of the area has his office there. Hiram Anderson, a good man. Listen to him. Report any problems to him. When your report is finished send it to him, he'll send it on."

"When you get to Lake Harbor be sure to check in with Sheriff Benjamin of Ottawa County and Chief Lawrence of the Lake Harbor city police. State cops can't get anything done if the locals don't cooperate. Damn patchwork system, we have to check in with the locals every time we turn around. Keep them happy, right?"

With a nod the director dismissed Preston. As he turned to leave he heard the director shout at Leona to bring him a cup of coffee. On the way out he stood aside to let the secretary deliver the coffee. He waited at her desk as she came back. She handed him a voucher ticket and bumped into him gently. Their hands touched and she smiled. For a moment Preston felt her soft shoulder and smelled her spicy fragrance.

Outside he lit a Camel as he walked slowly back to the empty barracks. While he savored the smoke, he wondered if the touch of her hand had been lingering, the bump of their bodies purposeful? Or was it all his wishful thinking? Did Leona like to dance?

Chapter 8

"That miserable wife-beating son-of-bitch."

Mary Fulton reacted loudly to Dorothea's news about the abuse of Florence Gunderson. Dorothea had just gotten into Mary's sporty Ford Club Coupe in front of the rooming house.

"He beats up on the sweetest woman in the world," Mary raved. "The rat. If I knew the phone number of that prizefighter I'd give him a call. Get him over here to go a few rounds with Otto." She struck the steering wheel in anger and frustration. "You know, the cute fighter we saw on the newsreel at the movies. Curly hair and he's been in pictures. What's his name?"

"Baer. Max Baer, Mary." Dorothea responded patiently. "He was champion once."

"Yeah, that's him. Cute, big and hits like a mule." She smacked her fist against the palm of her hand.

Dorothea nodded but her assent wasn't very enthusiastic. She shared Mary's rage but she felt only frustration now. Ever since Mildred had gossiped with her at the butcher shop she'd been seeking some way to punish Otto, some fitting vengeance. But she'd been unable to find a chastisement that would not backfire on Florence.

Mary turned off the car motor. "Just a sec. I got a tire iron in the trunk. Let's get it and go over there. See how Otto likes being on the receiving end."

Clasping the hand that held the car keys Dorothea spoke softly. "All day I've been thinking about Otto and wanting to give him what he's got coming. I'd enjoy whacking him with a tire iron, Mary. But think what Florence would have to put up with afterward."

"Yeah," Mary replied. "He'd take it out on her."

"He would." She perked up. "Let's think about Florence. About now I bet she could use a few drinks and a laugh with friends." Mary put the key in the ignition and fired up the engine.

"You're a smart cookie, Miss Dolan." Mary put the car in gear and slowly let out the clutch. "Let's go on over and get Florence. Sore leg or not she needs a night out. We can help her out to the car. Let's do it." Her jaw was set.

"Otto's not going to like this one bit," Dorothea said softly.

Mary eased her foot off the gas and looked at her friend. "Yeah, he might not."

Dorothea smiled. "You really got a tire iron in the trunk?"

Mary pressed down on the gas and the Ford accelerated as the women laughed.

Fueled by nips from Mary's hip flask they arrived at the Gunderson house in high spirits. Mary leaned on the horn. "That'll wake Otto up," she announced.

Three small faces appeared at the front window. The children recognized Dorothea and waved before they scurried away to be replaced by Otto's square head topped with a crew cut.

Dorothea waited until she was joined by Mary and in step they strode to the house. In response to Mary's knock Otto's muffled voice ordered them to "Go away". "Florence don't feel so good," he added.

When she knocked again he opened the door a crack. "Go away. I told you . . . ." The sharp toe of Mary's pump wedged into the space and shoulders against the door together they pushed him back. "Thanks, we will come in for a moment." Dorothea announced.

Mary fixed the husband with a venomous stare and called out. "Florence, honey, where are you?"

"Back here, Mary. In the back bedroom." Her voice sounded tired and weak.

Otto stood in the hallway, big and unmoving like a statue. On his jowly face confusion alternated with anger. Mary and Dorothea pushed past him and went down the hallway to join their friend. After a short argument from Florence they helped her up out of bed. While Mary helped Florence get dressed, Dorothea went to the front room and played with the children.

Aided by a cane and leaning on Mary's arm Florence made it out to the backseat of the car. Dorothea hung back to make sure Otto presented no problem.

She opened the front door of the house to leave but shut it. Dorothea and Otto were alone in the front door hallway. She looked into his bleary eyes and saw fear there. In a flash she knew what she could do to help Florence.

Otto turned to face Dorothea, feigning anger. She stepped closer and smiled up at him. He stunk of liquor, sweat and fear. When he worked, the guy was a substitute clerk at the city water works. He acted like he was King Kong and the people around him allowed him to behave like that. She'd put some fear in him.

"Otto, I was just thinking. Mary's husband is a big shot with the railroad and has a lot of tough guys working for him. I've got sailors staying at my rooming house. They're pretty tough too. Those fellows make good friends. Know what I mean?" She winked at him. She was stretching the truth but he didn't know that. The angry glare was gone and his mouth hung open.

She patted his arm. "Good friends. They'd do anything for us. If someone, anyone was hurting someone we liked they'd come over to talk to that someone. It would be a very serious talk. Know what I mean?"

As Otto listened his broad face grew pale.

"I don't know," Dorothea went on, "but I'd guess that once those fellows got angry, really upset it'd be the devil to get them to stop. They'd even hold you while someone went to work on you." With the flat of her hand she made a chopping motion and stared at his groin.

She waited a long moment, "Know what I mean?"

His eyes nervously avoided her level gaze. He nodded once quickly.

The car horn sounded.

Dorothea backed out the door. "Well, goodnight Otto. I told your oldest to help the others get ready for bed. You rest well too. Don't wait up; we'll probably be late."

By the time she got to Mary's car, Florence had had a couple of sips and her leg was feeling better. The three women sang Ukelele Ike's latest hit about wishing on a star and when they arrived at the party they were feeling absolutely wonderful.

The welcome Florence got at Mona Newton's made her feel even better. The arrival of Florence energized the gathering. The pinochle cards remained untouched on the game table as the drinks flowed and the laughter rose.

Stretched out on Mona's new pink loveseat, leg cushioned on a pillow, Florence was served highballs by the other women. After a few hours she waved Dorothea over to the loveseat. "Sure am glad I came. Had a great time." She handed her glass to her friend. "But I got to throw cold water on the party. I'm worried about my kids. And Alex, my youngest, had a headache. He's kind of delicate and might be coming down with something. Would you ask Mary if you'all could take me home?"

ꝫ ꝫ ꝫ

After helping Florence to her front door Dorothea and Mary waited to make sure the Gunderson house remained quiet.

"Had a short chat with Otto before we went to the party, maybe he's seen the light," Dorothea said as they sat in silent darkness. Giving into her friend's questions she told Mary what she'd told Otto.

Her friend's reaction was to drive away from the house before both of them broke into raucous laughter. "O, dear lord, Dorothea, you're going to be the death of me."

"Let's hope Otto believes me and stops hitting Florence. Otherwise I'll have to get me some tough guys and a butcher knife."

"Miss Dolan, I'll bet all the gold in Fort Knox that once you gave him that evil eye look of yours he was convinced. Scary. It's a sure thing he'll believe you. I do!"

They were still laughing when Mary drove down to the beach and they watched moonlight play on the waves. Then they were silent.

"Dorothea, don't you get lonely? Sometimes don't you just want a man around?"

"Mary, I can't say that on cold nights I don't get lonely. I miss having a man to hold me and talk to me. But then, truth be told, we'd just get into an argument." She rubbed her eyes. "I'm getting settled in my ways, had gentlemen friends and a marriage. I don't know that I have the strength to try romance again."

"Yeah, I understand what you're saying. I see what Florence goes through and I wonder why we do it, why we take all that crap from them." She wiped her eyes with a handkerchief. Then she spoke as if to the distant sound of the waves.

"Jerome makes a pretty good living. We're lucky, better off than most. Dammit, why isn't that enough for him. As a district supervisor for the Grand Trunk he travels a lot." She inhaled and held her breath for a moment. "Well, he's got a floozy in Detroit. Seems the only time he smiles and talks to me nice is when he's packing for a trip. It's the guilt making him pleasant."

She sighed, "For a day or two when he's back he's quiet. Doesn't yell at me so much." The surf hissed against the beach.

"I'm forty-two, an old lady and I don't care," Mary spoke around the unlit cigarette she'd just put between her lips. "As long as Jerome pays the bills I'd rather he was frisky with her than me. Let's have a drink." She handed her silver flask to Dorothea and wiped her eyes again.

Dorothea had had several drinks at the party and protested that she was tired and needed to get up early. "Your roomers, huh?" Dorothea nodded as Mary broke her cigarette and tossed it out the window. She started the automobile. "You take care of them like they are your family."

"Yeah, Mary, you're right. I do and I guess they are."

When they pulled up in front of the rooming house Dorothea got out of the car carefully. The alcohol was making her feel a bit unsteady. She said goodnight to her friend in carefully modulated tones. But she stumbled on the stairs as Mary drove away.

There was no difficulty getting the key into the keyhole and opening the heavy front door. The sight inside the house startled her.

In the foyer, huddled on the bottom stair in the shadows was what appeared to be a pile of clothes. As she watched it moved, and Alma's face appeared from the folds of a blue wool robe.

Dorothea muffled her small cry and said, "Goodness, you gave me a start. Alma, what are you doing sitting there? You'll catch a cold."

Alma sat up and pulled her robe tightly about her skinny body. "Dorothea, I'm so worried. Max is sick, bad. Gus is out. I'm all alone here." Tears glinted in her eyes. "He's been moaning all evening. I tapped on his door and I don't think he knew who it was. He called me Mama and then he cursed. I was afraid to go in, Dorothea, he was groaning so loud."

Dorothea straightened up and felt the pleasant fogginess of the liquor leave her. "Don't worry, Alma. Go on up to your room and I'll take care of Max. I'll get rid of the pain for him. You go on to bed. Everything will be all right."

Alma's eyes seemed to glow, "Oh, Dorothea, you take such good care of us."

      ટ ટ ટ

Dorothea went into Max's room quietly. The old man was on his bed breathing stertorously. Occasionally he would stop and moan but then the painful breaths would resume.

It was time for the nicotine. It was just medicine. A little shot of the stuff in his vein. No pain.

Once in a while there was nausea. She didn't mind cleaning up. It was the least she could do. His pain would be over.

Chapter 9

"**S**till a cop. I'm still a cop." He grinned as the refrain ran through his brain. Preston promised himself that there'd be no solitary sandwich for supper, no dull book to read in the barracks tonight. No dismissal. That fat phony had given him an assignment. Preston had landed on his feet. From here on out he'd control his drinking. In Lake Harbor he'd work hard and get his career back on track.

Scarcely aware of the change in scenery, Preston walked off the State Police grounds and into downtown East Lansing. The heat of the day had eased a bit and he found himself across the street from the White Pine Restaurant and Lounge.

He recalled hearing Sims or one of the other young troopers bragging about this place. Preston recalled that the young cops had placed it high on the two main recreational requirements: generous drinks and good-looking women. Both were pleasures he'd been without for too long.

Edith had never been able to comprehend male needs. He'd loved his wife and daughter but needed to get out of the house and relax once in a while. She refused to give him the space he needed. There was no reason for her to worry, he'd always returned. That was ancient history. As a divorced man with a revived career he could do what he wanted. And this was the night he would have some fun, then he'd get back to work.

When he stopped across the street from the restaurant a man in a cap and filthy clothes rose from his seat on the sidewalk, straightened his jacket and limped toward Preston. Muttering unintelligibly he grasped a few pencils in his left hand and held them out toward Preston. A scarred and misshapen right hand tapped the cardboard sign tied round his neck with string.

VETRAN

PLEEZ

HELP

The three words had been printed with a red crayon. Bright yellow paint on the proffered pencils contrasted with the dirty gray of his shirt.

This close to the panhandler the stench was shocking. Preston felt in his pockets for spare change. He found some pennies and a nickel. The coins rattled in the tin cup the panhandler held out, hooked on a finger of his deformed right hand. He croaked "Bless You, sir" and patted the sign. Preston turned away and hurried across the street.

The man's stink was still in his nose. The two of them had been in the same war. Maybe the derelict had been a Marine; perhaps he'd been at the battle of Belleau Woods with Preston. He pushed through the brass and glass doors into the foyer. The air was fresh with the clean scents of food and drink and lovely women. Finley had told Preston he did not have to be in Lake Harbor until Monday. A little partying tonight and then right back to the straight and narrow.

He moved into the bright restaurant. Soft carpet, cool marble, coat check counter, white pillars by the entrance to the dining room. Two steps down into the huge room and he waited.

Before him on the circular dance floor couples moved in time to the music. There were still some folks doing all right in these tough times. It sure was a long way from that beggar out on the street to this place.

"Sir?" the maitre d'hotel addressed him and waited. He stared at Preston's suit and with a slight sneer averted his eyes to the menu held in his manicured, patient hands.

"I'll just have a drink." He was hungry but at the last minute his nerve failed. He didn't want to sit out there in the sea of comfortable people at small tables. Not yet anyway, a few drinks and then he'd eat. With a small bow and a gesture toward the bar the maître d' left Preston and flashed a smile at the couple behind him.

Preston climbed the steps to the mezzanine bar. The stool felt comfortable, a natural place for him. He lit a cigarette and looked out across the dance floor. The band was playing the Guy Lombardo arrangement of "Enjoy Yourself."

Just the right tune; in response to the bartender Preston ordered a bottle of Blatz beer and a shot of Four Roses whiskey. He'd have just one shot and then stick to beer the rest of the evening. Walt's words about controlling his intake of liquor were firmly in his memory. As long as he remembered the advice he'd control his drinking.

He tossed the shot down and felt the warmth spread through his body. Head buzzing he shivered and poured a glass of beer. Very carefully he took a long celebratory drink. Life was fine.

The bartender seemed to read his mind.

"Sir, would you care for something to eat? At the bar we serve a very nice roast beef sandwich."

Perfect. After another long drink of beer Preston wiped his lips and nodded. He had made a wise choice to come here.

The bartender was right. It was a tasty sandwich and Preston dispatched it promptly. Then he was ready for another beer while he planned the rest of the evening. Watching the people and hearing their chatter, the syncopation of the music complemented the faint electric vibration in his head. Beyond the diners, couples moved and dipped in time to the music.

He was disappointed when he spotted no unescorted women, but not far from where he sat was a young couple. The cute blonde looked bored as she pretended to listen to her date. Her eyes surveyed the crowd as she fiddled with a pack of cigarettes. Her partner was young guy, tall and slender, not bad looking with curly brown hair. The fellow seemed wrapped up in himself as he chattered away fascinated with his own words as he gestured excit-edly. Curly stopped talking for a moment and the woman nodded and started in on her own tale. The fellow interrupted and spun out another story. She shut up, frowned and took a sip of her drink.

From his place at the bar Preston could tell what the blonde desired. Yet her date at the same table wasn't even aware. Preston finished his beer, ordered another. Before long she'd go to the lady's room. Just to get away from his chatter, for something to do. When she did he'd slide over and find out if she really wanted to have a good time. He bet he knew what her answer would be.

"Here. Let me light that for you." She looked up at Preston and held the cigarette to her mouth waiting. He struck the match and held it to the Chesterfield.

"Thanks," she said and waited to see what would happen next. She was returning from the ladies room. Preston had intercepted her where the short hallway from the rest rooms ended at the dance floor.

"Want to dance?" Preston blew out the match and dropped it.

"I don't know."

"While you're deciding let's have a little dance." He took her elbow and stepped toward the dance floor. She was smaller, more petite than she had seemed when he saw her from the bar.

"No, better not." She pulled back.

"Something wrong?"

She gestured with her chin toward the table where her date waited. Preoccupied he seemed to be wrapped up in thinking of more things to say as he fiddled with his drink. "My boyfriend, he'd be upset. He's got a temper."

"He own you?"

"Well, no. I'm my own boss." She shrugged. "But we're almost engaged."

"Consider this a last fling."

She giggled and tossed her head showing her yellow tresses prettily. "He gets jealous."

"Do you give him reason to?"

Laughing again she did not answer.

"What's your name?"

"I don't know if I should encourage you."

"Encourage him how, Dawn?"

Her tall, skinny boyfriend had come up behind Preston. Neither person had seen him. Anger blazed in boyfriend's eyes.

Preston touched the boy's arm. It would not do for him to get arrested because of a fight. "No need to get upset fellow. I was just having a chat with the lady."

"Get your hands off me, you, you, masher." Dawn pushed Preston in a sudden demonstration of outrage.

Were the situation not so potentially dangerous Preston would have laughed in boyfriend's red face. He didn't and kept his eyes trained on curly's hands in case boyfriend started throwing punches. Even in high-class joints Preston knew that there were bouncers paid to remain invisible until something like this started up. They were probably closing in on the scene right now.

"I don't like guys pawing you, Dawn. I told you that before." His voice was shrill his hands were clenched and held against his chest.

"There you are, dear. Here, you left your hat at the bar." Preston turned at the sound of a female voice and looked into Leona's smile as he accepted his fedora. "I hope I didn't keep you waiting long, Preston. Let's go somewhere and have a drink."

"Please excuse us." Leona smiled at boyfriend and his Dawn as she led Preston to the restaurant exit.

Part Two ⸻

August 1940

Chapter 10

"**I** was so pleased to talk to you on the phone Miss Dolan," Mordechai said as he sat down. They were alone in the kitchen since the roomers were in the front room. Apparently they were enjoying themselves since laughter and piano tunes drifted into the room. "It was fortunate to talk to you."

"Please call me Dorothea, Mister McNeil. I always answer the phone in this house. That way I can screen the calls and protect my guests from unwanted calls."

"How very thoughtful of you, Dorothea."

"Would you care for some coffee or perhaps a cup of tea?"

"Absolutely delightful, a cup of tea would be very welcome indeed." Dorothea rose slowly from her seat by the kitchen table. She was moving slowly since it had been a very busy day. As she put the kettle on the stove and assembled the cup, and saucer and put some ginger snaps on a plate, she had to smile at herself. Just this past weekend she had sat in the dark in this very room and wept with frustration and desperation because her rooming house was empty. And now the rooms were filling up again. She put the hot tea pot and the dishes on a tray and turned back to Mordechai.

"You said on the phone, Mister McNeil that you were interested in a room here?"

"Yes, indeed, I have heard good things about your house." He waited as Dorothea poured his cup full and then he carefully added three teaspoons of sugar to the drink He took a sip and beamed at her. "The tea exemplifies the favorable testimony Miss – Forgive me, Dorothea. Both excellent." He smiled beatifically at her and Dorothea thought how like a short caricature of Santa Claus her new candidate for a room was. But looks weren't all.

"Mordechai, I usually require a recommendation from an applicant. I understand you cannot give me one."

"Forgive me, Dorothea, I am a traveling salesman. Have sold dining materials – silverware, dishes and such – to hotels in the East. As you can see, I am no longer young." A genteel smile preceded another sip of tea. "I will travel a little in Michigan selling my wares but I want to settle down. Your abode seems a nice place, no, an ideal place for me to retire. I certainly hope that you will accept my request."

"Since you have no recommendation I fear I must require a full week's rent in advance, you'll understand."

"Absolutely. I am prepared to advance that amount. May I consider myself a roomer and you my landlord?" Before he heard Dorothea's reply he had taken his wallet from his jacket, taken out some greenbacks and set them on the table. "Champion," Mordechai said and clapped his pudgy hands together. Raising his teacup in the air like a trophy he then drained it and sat beaming at her.

"When will you move in, Mordechai?"

"I am presently residing at the Railroad Hotel, a place that, shall I be politic? A residence that does not allow a light sleeper like me much rest."

Dorothea shook her head. "You will find your room clean

and freshly aired. And I can promise you that –" The singing grew louder now. "Despite the present evidence. I can promise you quiet nights."

Mordechai rose from his chair and fussily arranged his jacket and trousers. "Ah, Dorothea, one more question."

She stood facing him. "Yes?"

"Though my business will lessen over time I will still be receiving, for a few months at least, some business related mail. What are the arrangements?"

"Mordechai, there is no reason for concern. The mail is received in the slot in the front door. All of it falls into a locked metal box. I have the key. I will deliver your mail to your room."

"I see. Thank you, madam." He shook her hand. On the way out he dwelt a moment at the front door and ran his hand over the metal box. Dorothea closed the door after him and returned to the kitchen.

Here it was Monday, August 26, 1940 and a month or so past she'd had no guests at all on the second floor and she'd been fearful that she might have to move herself. She cleaned up the kitchen and then turned off the lights and sat in the dark. The window over the sink looked out onto the lake. In the pool of night darkness she could make out ship lights slowly moving across the waters. From the front room there came a burst of laughter reminding her that when Mordechai moved in tomorrow five of the rooms would be taken. Only one remained empty and even with that she figured she'd put a little money aside.

Poor Max had died after a long, painful decline. Gus had moved out to get married; the old fool. She felt the most sorrow for Alma, poor, dear little Alma. The voices had returned to torture her. She started drinking again and one day, after an all day bender, she'd made a big ruckus in a dockside tavern. Reports were that she broken some furniture, glasses and the big mirror behind the bar; a lot of damage by a small woman. The proprietor of the tavern complained to the Chamber of Commerce and that august body complained to the city of Lake Harbor. Large men in uniform from the Michigan Asylum for the Insane at Kalamazoo came for her. They showed Alma and Dorothea a committal order signed by a judge and then bound the struggling Alma in straps and secured her in a seat in a van for the drive to the Asylum.

Dorothea could only stand and watch the vehicle drive away while the little woman yelled.

"The golden flicker of the fireflies, the gleam of love light in your lovely eyes." In the dark kitchen Dorothea imagined hearing Alma's quavering soprano singing the song she'd heard on the radio months ago. At least she had been able to help Max and the poor man no longer suffered.

She dabbed at the moisture in her eyes and suddenly was aware that the singing and piano playing had been replaced by loudly arguing voices. The words weren't clear but back and forth yelling was clearly motivated by hot tempers. After taking a moment to catch her breath and patience she eased open one of the sliding doors and stepped into the front room.

Clement Schultz, tall and skinny, held out his arms in a classic pugilistic pose. He circled Nils Nilsson, a short man built along the lines of a fireplug. Both snarled and snapped but neither closed the distance between them.

"What going on here?" Dorothea demanded. Beryl Richards, another new guest rose from the sofa and tattled.

"Dorothea, they're going to fight, to hit each other," she said, an edge of excitement in her voice. Her dear friend, Minnie Quinton, turned on her seat at the piano, she was a retired music teacher, and watched the fracas with a slight smile.

"Let the old fools have at it," Minnie suggested. "A little excitement for a change."

Dorothea took a step into the room. Everyone waited for her words. "I agree with you Minnie," she said. "But they might break some of the furniture, bleed on the carpet."

"Dorothea," Clement pled. "He said I was a Nazi."

"Never did," Nils said as he let his arms fall to his side. "I said Germans were acting like Nazis. They marched into Denmark and took over my homeland." He offered the last statement as a bit of historical explanation to Dorothea.

"I never did," said Clement in an affronted tone.

"OK, that's enough you two. Minnie, thank you for the musical evening, it was very nice.. You and Beryl can rest well." As the two old women headed for the stairs together, Dorothea turned to the sheepish men to address them. "Clement, Nils, be assured now that this is a respectable establishment. It's not like that Hardy's Tavern, that terrible place I found you. If you'd like to return there to drink too much and sleep at a table then you'll continue to disrupt our evenings. This will never happen again. Is that clear." The men nodded their white heads and went to the stairs to go up to their rooms. Clement stood aside to let Nils go up the stairs first.

Dorothea allowed the stern expression on her face to relax into a smile and tidied up the front room. She brushed off the sofa with her hand and plumped the cushions on the chair. There was some dust to be wiped from the piano with a corner of her apron. Back in the kitchen she turned on the lights and surveyed the room. There were a few dishes that she rapidly washed and set in the drainer. Oatmeal in the mornings, she planned. The weather was warm but her charges liked a breakfast that would stick to their ribs.

It was still rather early but her work was done; she'd give herself a quick cold cream facial and go to bed early. She had a foot on the first step of the front stairway when the phone rang. She hurried to answer, afraid the shrill jangling would disturb her roomers.

Chapter 11

It seemed to Preston that the gas pump would not stop ringing as it filled up the tank on his department issued 1938 Ford Coupe. He'd driven all round this town and the countryside looking for the people who'd been witnesses to the bank robbery seven years ago. August 18, 1933 the crime had been done. Here he was almost exactly seven years later trying to find the witnesses to interview. The pump bell stopped dinging and the attendant returned the nozzle to the pump and hurried to the front to clean the windshield.

Preston got out of his car and shrugged out of his jacket. It felt like he was in a jungle or something. He'd been perspiring all day. He had a list of names of the witnesses to the robbery and he had a map of the area. But it seemed to him that a committee of monkeys had drawn the map and that every one of the witnesses had moved to the North Pole. He'd spent weeks looking.

He threw down a sour tasting cigarette end and spat. No, it wasn't only that those people moved or that the map was inaccurate, it had begun to go bad when he had met with that dope Finley. That weekend of booze and sex with Leona had started his problems. He'd arrived in Grand Rapids and talked with that Anderson guy and didn't remember much. In Lake Harbor he'd been even drunker. Met with some police sergeant, Spivak, was his name. Seemed like a nice fellow but Preston rejected offers of help. He would get his career back on track all by himself.

"That'll be $3.50, sir. Would you like me to check your tires?"

Preston looked at the smiling young attendant hopelessly. He knew that his frustration would lead him back into one of the taverns near the cheap hotel where he stayed. He knew too that Finley's patience would soon run out. His chance for a revived career was melting away in this August heat. If he didn't swallow his pride and ask for some help he was done for. "Naw, that'll be all," he handed the young man money. "I won't be going far."

~ ~ ~

Preston slowly entered the office of Sergeant Spivak, the shift commander of the Lake Harbor police department, and sat down. The detective could see the concern and sympathy on the thin face of the city cop. Preston knew he must look like hell. He was half drunk and he hadn't had a decent night's sleep in a week.

Spivak chuckled softly. Preston looked at him feeling defensive. Had he made a mistake coming here for help?

"Sorry, I think that sneak thief Bentz has got all of us running around like chickens with their heads cut off. He's a real con that one is."

"Yes, he is and he sure has me running around," Preston admitted wearily.

"Well, just relax, Preston, my friend." He pulled open a bottom drawer of his scarred desk and took out a bottle of Scotch.

"Your problem is over. We'll have a little drink and in the morning I'll introduce you to a department treasure. Patrolman Pflam, Noah, is his christened name. Other officers call him Pflim-Pflam cause he's so good at getting out of hard work. He could have been a successful flim-flam man, you know, a con artist. But he's a good soul, near retirement and most important he knows the city and the countryside like the back of his hand. He'll help you find the people and you can interview them, OK?"

Preston returned the smile and reached for the drink. Spivak raised his glass and said, "Here's to the criminals who keep us in business."

"Thanks so much, I really owe you for this one," Preston said as he set the empty glass on the desk.

"Well, now that we got you sorted out, give me a minute. I'll keep it short." Spivak waited for Preston's assent and then went on. "Except for the dock area Lake Harbor is a peaceful town. People move here for the quiet. We've been having a devil of a time lately. There's been eight cars stolen in the last six months. I've been in this job fifteen years and the average might be one stolen car a year. Captain Lawrence, the chief of police, is being badgered by the city administration like you wouldn't believe. You got any ideas?"

"I worked traffic for the State Police for years and that pattern is pretty clear. Look in the high schools."

"We've got one named Lake Harbor Senior High School."

"All right, you have a young looking officer, send him over there to hang around and listen. I'll bet you get some leads pretty quick."

Spivak gestured with the whiskey bottle again. Preston held up his hand in refusal. It was smooth liquor but it was going straight to his head. He'd better get some rest. Spivak nodded, "Thanks. That verifies what I guessed. We've nailed a couple of kids gone bad and recovered some of the cars."

"But?"

"Yeah, but, we've never found a Cadillac and two Packards."

Preston nodded and pressed his burning eyes with his thumbs. "They're the bigger, heavier cars. Hold more men and can take more bullet hits. Kids prefer Ford V8s, like mine, they're faster. You get a bigger thrill." He stopped to yawn.

"You're dead on your feet. I'll give you directions to the best rooming house in town. We'll call it a night."

"You're right but let me add this. It could be that a car-stealing gang has moved to your fair town. They could be working with bank robbers. The local gang snatches autos, makes sure the motor and transmission are working perfectly. They sell them for a very nice price and the bank robbers have a vehicle for their heist. I'll bet some of those three cars you can't find are hidden nearby waiting for sale."

Spivak nodded. "Lord knows this Depression has emptied out farms and orchards all round Lake Harbor. Any one of them could be a hiding place for those thieves. Cops just stumble around howling about their jurisdiction." He smiled at Preston. "Thanks and I've kept you long enough. I'll call ahead, it's an easy place to find."

"That's good. I've not been very successful finding my way around."

"When I get through with this Bentz investigation maybe I can get permission to help you with these cars. If there is a gang operating in the neighborhood I have some ideas about how to bring them down."

"Right, thanks. I'll give Dorothea a call. Usually she takes old folks as roomers. If I ask her maybe she'll give you a room. It'll be quiet and she sets the best table in town."

Chapter 12

For the second time this evening Dorothea welcomed a gentleman into her kitchen. Mordechai McNeil had been welcome as a new boarder. Preston Duhamel was welcome on the same basis but, she had to admit, some other aspects of the man sitting at the small table were intriguing. He was quite good looking and he lent a young face for her to see at breakfast among the wrinkles and beards. Though she might flirt a bit Dorothea was concerned as well. Poor man looked like he might have been ill. She knew how to take care of the folks who came to her house.

"Mister Duhamel, there's cold boiled potatoes, a slice of pork, some bread and butter. The coffee is hot, strong too. Would you care for tea instead?

She pointed to the meal laid out on the small kitchen table sensing a surprising nervousness in her voice. Perhaps she was overtired, it had been a long day and those old fools had made her angry. "When Milton Spivak told me your name I thought you might like tea. I can make you some." Dorothea laughed uneasily. Did she sound a bit, well, prejudiced?

Preston stood at the kitchen entrance holding his hat and looking about. "Thank you, coffee will be fine." He sat down at the place she indicated. She turned away and rattled some dishes in the sink as she rinsed them. Preston was staring at her; did she really look so old and tired?

He sliced up the potato and ate a bite. "My grandpere Octave was a tea drinker. He came south from Quebec City looking for work. My father Pierre and I were born in the States. We lost the habit of drinking tea, now drink coffee. I was born here in Michigan, in Detroit."

Shyness under control she looked back at her newest boarder. "Like Sergeant Spivak you too are a policeman?"

"Yes, I'm a detective with the state police."

"Oh, the state police. Didn't know there was a state police. Shows my ignorance, Mr. Duhamel. Or should I call you Detective Duhamel?"

"Please, Miss Dolan, call me Preston."

"All right, Preston and you must call me Dorothea."

Having established a modicum of familiarity she was again overcome by unease. Was this man here to investigate her? He put another morsel of potato in his mouth, she turned back to the sink to put away the supper dishes. She liked to leave the kitchen tidy and she needed a good excuse to look away from Preston.

"Emil Spivak is a good friend." In the silence Dorothea found herself chattering away. "He comes by to visit once a week or so and when he has time he stays to have breakfast." Thank goodness she hadn't said anything outrageous. She handled the dishes carefully. Her hands were unsteady, was she that tired?

She stole a glance at Preston. Poor man appeared tired; there was a dark and pinched look to his face as if he had recently recovered from an illness. He limped and when he sat down he favored his left leg. He couldn't be here to trap her. She hoped he would find the room comfortable and sleep well.

☙ ☙ ☙

Preston woke and listened without moving. Why had he wakened? Had his name been called? He waited and heard nothing more. There was a small window, Preston saw it was still dark outside; there was a pre-dawn stillness in the air. Resolved, he threw back the blankets, shivering as the chill of a new day touched him. The cold made his head throb as he dressed.

The hallway was dark. He felt his suit coat on a wire hanger on the door knob. Dorothea had stayed up to iron his suit so he'd make a good impression working with Pflam. She was quite a woman. From one of the rooms came the sound of coughing and sleepy muttering. He remembered the way to the toilet and then went to the stairs, illuminated by a tiny night-light. He stepped on the sides of the treads so that they did not creak. The clock in the big room at the foot of the stairs was lit by light from the street. It was still early. He had time for a walk before breakfast.

The cold breeze off the lake penetrated his jacket. He walked briskly along the nearly empty streets to warm up. A dairy truck slowly passed him. Against the barely lit sky the tall rectangular vehicle reminded Preston of a large casket. It stopped, and the white clad milkman raced from the truck to leave a bottle of milk on a dark porch.

Preston decided he would see the lake, walk on the beach and then return for breakfast. The exercise and the fresh air would help him get sorted out. Yesterday he hadn't done a very good job of handling things. He'd gotten frustrated and then he'd begun stopping for a drink. All he had to do was ask for some help. Spivak would help him out and he'd get that report to Anderson right away.

His thoughts wandered back to the time in East Lansing after he'd talked with Finley. Leona! Lordy, what a weekend they'd had. Did Dorothea like to dance? Funny, when Spivak mentioned the rooming house he'd imagined some tight-lipped old crone. Boy, had he been wrong.

He should know by now that Four Roses whiskey was not a good drink for him. Stick to beer, or mixed drinks, keep track of the amount he drank. He made a mental note to search the car for empty bottles. It would not do for the local police to imagine he was a drunk.

The shore curved gradually to the northwest, and the slow dawn was so clear that he imagined he could see all the way to Canada. A tanker headed west, probably for Milwaukee. A quarter mile or less away there was a marina made up of a floating walkway to which two ranks of boats were moored.

Though he was headed into the cold morning breeze, he walked to the marina to see the varicolored boats buck against the moorings. Most were small rowboats but there were a few larger motor vessels. Bobbing on waves beyond the boats, a flock of ducks watched him and warily paddled away.

A mile or two along the shore he glimpsed a jetty made of loose rocks enclosed by heavy metal sheeting. Where the structure ended out in the lake there was a tower with a rotating light to warn vessels away from the shore and toward the entrance to the harbor. He looked into the deep, dark waters and a chill came into his bones. Turning away shivering, he made his way back toward the house. Did Dorothea walk along the beach, gaze at the lights flickering in the darkness? He would like to walk with her.

To his left a wooden rowboat had been pulled up on the beach. It was propped on its side by some rocks. In the protected space beneath the boat a dark figure moved and moaned. A guy out of work like that one he'd given some pennies to outside the restaurant last night. Preston shivered and this time it was from dread. He was not all that far from the guy under the boat. Were Preston to lose his job it would not be long before he would be sleeping alongside that fellow.

The walk had helped; he was feeling much better, healthy and clean. Every morning he'd get up early. He'd walk through the sand, get into shape and strengthen his hip. Preston turned and retraced his steps. He ran a few steps. Best not to do too much since his hip was still delicate. It was time to go back to the house, warm up and have some breakfast.

He used the key Dorothea had given him to open the front door and let himself in. The large front room was warm and no other guests had come down yet though he heard noise in the kitchen. On the hall table he found a day old newspaper and took it to read in a comfortable upholstered chair across the room from the upright piano.

∾   ∾   ∾

Up a bit early; that wasn't unusual for Dorothea. She liked to get an early start on the day. The clear sky promised a fine day. Putting on her makeup, staring at herself in the mirror, Dorothea realized her thoughts were wandering into places she'd not visited often lately. Her thoughts were giddily fixed on a man. She was humming and she was thinking of Preston.

The realization was so shocking that she interrupted her preparations, went into her bedroom and sat in the chair where she did her sewing. In the past when perplexed she'd sew and talk to Grannie Quinn. Even if she found no answer to the pressing problem the anxieties were usually alleviated.

Hands folded in her lap, eyes closed, she posed the question to herself: What was going on?

The answer readily came: She was getting sweet on a fellow. By now she should be familiar with her romantic disposition.

There should be a fire alarm going off in her head. Those feelings were dangerous. Every time in the past she'd felt this way she'd gotten into trouble.

Preston was handsome and seemed to be in need of care. Was he lonely too or was that her imagination? Though Preston did not have a mustache, he reminded her of Philippe. She'd met Philippe in Hollywood. He'd been in very small parts in a few movies. He too had needed someone to care for him. They'd been married and for a short time it had been a heavenly match. Dorothea knew she was a sucker for lost puppies. When the money had run out so had Philippe. She had taken care of him but it wasn't enough.

Be careful! The silent warning to herself was urgent. She was older now and weary of the challenge and dance of love. That music was familiar and the memories were dear. Yes, she agreed. And romance was so sweet. She rose to smooth her dress. There was the batter to prepare for griddlecakes. Work would settle her down.

Chapter 13

After giving the batter a final stir with the wooden spoon, Dorothea tested the temperature of the griddle. Drops of water sizzled and danced across the iron surface. Everything was ready. The twelve circles of batter bubbled and browned while she stepped to the back stairs and announced that breakfast would soon be ready.

Deftly flipping the cakes a smile touched her mouth as the growing sounds of the roomers preparing for breakfast drifted down into the kitchen. Beryl and Minnie gossiped happily starting their day like they always did: as a kind of joyful adventure. Holding hands as the best of friends they greeted Mordechai McNeil after Dorothea introduced them. Short and pudgy Mordechai immediately captured the ladies' hearts when he kissed their hands. He pulled out the chairs for them but before he sat down Dorothea felt him watching her. Strange man, she thought.

The deep voices of Nils and Clement in bickering argument did not assail the morning. Could the warning last night have had an effect on those rascals? If so her day would be a serene one.

Dorothea turned the griddlecakes, allowed them to fry a moment and scooped them onto the platter. Pouring out a new batch she suddenly sensed that something was amiss: there'd been no sound of the new roomer preparing for the day. Was he a quiet man, had he overslept?

She felt a pinch of disappointment. If he were sleeping in this morning he'd miss breakfast and she was proud of her pancakes. Each one was made with a pinch of crushed walnuts and she had added a few drops of vanilla to the batter.

Feelings would have to wait while she fed her people. Laden with the coffee pot, dishes and silverware she went into the dining room to set the table. Setting her load down on the table she decided to go in to the front room. She didn't remember if she'd tidied it up last night. The glare of the floor lamp and the rattle of newspaper surprised her. Preston was already up and ready for a meal. He raised his eyes to her as she uttered a soft exclamation of surprise.

"Sorry if I interrupted your reading. I didn't know you were down already."

"Just looking at old news," he smiled and tossed the paper onto the side table as he rose. "Thanks for pressing my jacket and trousers. I was too tired to get my things from the hotel and then return here. You were very nice." He gestured dismissively at the newspapers. "Nothing there but politicians ranting and armies marching. That Hitler has taken over almost all of Europe." He stepped closer. "The smells from the kitchen are much more interesting." She felt a blush rising as Preston focused his gaze on her. "Breakfast smells delicious." The words were uttered softly.

She was impossible and blushed like a schoolgirl. "Thanks, hope it tastes as good as it smells. Come on in."

Slightly bowing he stood aside to allow her to go first. "May I help out?"

She hoped the hem of her dress was straight as she led the way into the dining room. "Well, you can help set the table if you wish."

Preston placed the silverware on each placemat on the table. "Woke early and took a walk on the beach."

Dorothea came back from the kitchen carrying a large platter of pancakes. "Walking on the beach in the morning is grand, isn't it. I like to watch the boats. Gracious, were dear Max still with us he'd be giving me what-for. 'They be ships, woman, ships. Boats has oars.'" She imitated the gruff voice of the old sailor who had roomed in her house until his quiet death. After explaining the memory to Preston she went on. "Anyway," she concluded, "I love to walk on the beach too."

She hurried back into the kitchen while Preston set plates on the table. Mordechai, Beryl and Minnie were in deep discussion at the table. After a quick look at herself in the little mirror she'd hung above the sink and arranging an errant lock of hair, she carried a pitcher of maple syrup back in to the dining room.

Preston had poured coffee into a cup and was sipping it. "Shall I fill the other cups, Dorothea?"

A little tingle ran through her as he used her name. "Preston, I think not."

"The old fellows like to pour their own coffee, right?"

She nodded and checked the table. The clomp of shoes on the stairs announced the imminent arrival of the guests. "Please sit here. I'll get the butter then we can eat. Help yourself."

Holding the butter dish and closing the heavy insulated door with a flick of the hip it came to her that she had seated Preston opposite her. Maybe this morning she'd be careful and not dribble syrup down her apron front.

Dorothea sat down as the roomers came down the back stairs through the kitchen and into the suddenly quiet dining room. Clement, tall and erect, slowly led the way. His face was pale, lips compressed in a thin line. He did not return Dorothea's greeting. Behind the old railroader came a somber Nils Nilsson. He waited while Clement sat down in his usual place at the end of the long rectangular table. Then the retired sailor carefully drew out his chair to the right of his erstwhile opponent. Neither man looked at Dorothea. Beryl and Minnie hurried to the table, greeting everyone with a smile. They let go of each other's hand to sit and help themselves to breakfast.

Mordechai, seated between the two women whispered something just loud enough for them to hear. They laughed and covered their mouths with their hands. He looked closely at Preston before he began to eat..

Before she began her own meal Dorothea took a deep breath, met Preston's look and introduced him to everyone.

"Ladies." He rose and bowed to greet Beryl and Minnie. They tittered. Then he shook hands with the men.

Clement quickly cut his pancakes into bite sizes, covered them with syrup and stuffed his mouth. Dorothea noticed that Nils was not eating. Was he ill?

Mordechai chewed, swallowed and carefully wiped his mouth. "Mr. Duhamel, I noticed a charming little park near here. I daresay you are familiar with the therapeutic benefits of a stroll after a fine breakfast. Would you care to walk with me?"

"Thank you, Mr. McNeil, another time. I will need to get to work today."

"Yes, another time. Would I be overly forward if I asked what is your line of work?"

"Not at all, Mr. McNeil. I am a state police detective and I'm investigating a bank robbery that occurred in Lake Harbor a few years ago.

"How exciting," Beryl breathed. A diminutive woman with a preference for blouses with high collars, she had been a school-teacher who'd cared for her father. She'd never married and when her father died she retired to live on the small inheritance left her.

Preston shook his head. "I'm afraid it is just boring routine. Find the witnesses, talk to them, record their testimony. Then I write a report. No excitement."

"The brave ones are always modest." Minnie's statement came out louder than she expected. Dorothea saw her blush intensely. She wondered if Minnie's long career as a music teacher had affected her hearing. Her statement had been made with a loud intensity and everyone, including the speaker, was surprised.

"Does all that talking while he's taking our tax money." Clement growled waving a fork in the direction of Preston.. Dorothea and the women aimed angry glances at him. But the atten-tion on him was suddenly displaced when Nils began weeping.

Nils took the handkerchief Dorothea offered him. She had jumped up and gone to him to hold his hand. Nils wept for another moment and then vigorously wiped his eyes and looked up at Dorothea. Clement had poured out a cup of coffee and slid the drink toward Nils.

"I'm sorry. Haven't cried in . . . well a long time. That letter you brought me yesterday evening Dorothea. Well, it was from Adalena my sister-in-law, from Denmark. She's married to my youngest brother Dag."

His voice broke and he sobbed but soon gained control.

"This past spring, April, the Nazis came, took over my homeland. Well, my brother is a politi, a cop like you Mr. Duhamel. Most Danish politi would not cooperate with the Nazi Gestapo. My brother and these other cops were involved in the resistance. Adalena wrote me that Dag and all his friends, all the cops he worked with have been arrested. They've been sent to a prison camp, Buchenwald. It's a terrible place. She's afraid she won't see him again. And there are four children to raise."

"They're not real Germans." Clement uttered his judgment as he banged the table with his fist. "Nazis are criminals."

Nils wiped away his tears, rose from the table and excused himself. He went into the front room followed by Clement. The two old men sat next to each other on the couch talking quietly.

No one seemed hungry now. Mordechai sipped his coffee while looking up and down the table. Beryl and Minnie held hands and gazed at their plates. Preston slowly chewed as he watched Dorothea return to her chair.

She moved the food on her plate around and put down her fork.

"Well," her voice was gentle, "we all must be kind and thoughtful with our friend Nils." She pushed her plate back. "Those poor children."

The phone rang.

Chapter 14

Dorothea spoke on the phone for a moment. "Preston," she waved to him. "It's for you."

A loud friendly voice greeted him. "Mr. Duhamel, sir, Noah Pflam. Sergeant Spivak assigned me to work with you."

"Morning, Noah, come by in an hour will you? I have a car and will do the driving. Need to get to know the city."

"Good plan, sir," Pflam concurred. "Don't drive, never acquired the knack. But I know the city well."

Three days later Preston waited at the curb for his assistant to arrive. In three days they had interviewed almost every person on the list given Preston by Inspector Finley's office. With luck today he'd finish the interrogations and soon he'd send the report off to Detective Anderson. Preston flipped his morning cigarette into the gutter and sighed. Pflam was always ten or fifteen minutes late.

The first time Pflam was tardy Preston had told him, "Just tell me where you live, I'll come by for you."

"Can't do that Mr. Duhamel." He stroked his moustache

with thumb and forefinger. "As one man to another, sir, it is like this. My sleeping arrangements vary. There are different opportunities, you might say."

Preston's revery was interrupted by a merry shout as Pflam rode up on his red Schwinn bicycle. "Reporting for duty sir."

He doffed his billed cap and jumped from his bike and carefully folded the white muslin duster he wore to protect his uniform.

Even from several feet away Preston caught the yeasty odor of beer on Pflam's breath. He wondered if he drank that stuff all the time. The man had at least two addictions.

"Morning; yesterday's interviews typed? In triplicate?" Preston's questions were terse. He wanted his report to be prompt and complete. He took the witness' testimony down in longhand and Pflam took the pages to a typist at the police station to be transcribed.

Pflam bounced on the toes of his polished boots. "Before I left the station last night, sir. All nice dark letters on snowy white paper, carbons and originals."

Opening the door of the Ford, Preston got in. "Very good, come on. Today I need to talk to the three bank employees who were there during the robbery. They are the last ones and I'd like to finish today."

He waited until Pflam was seated next to him.

"I'll draft my report while the typist works on today's interviews. In the morning I'll reread it. Hopefully I can send it to Detective Anderson in Grand Rapids tomorrow."

Pflam beamed and nodded. "And a fine report it will be, sir."

"Mister Duhamel, you appear a bit worn out."

He had just finished the last interview at the bank. Teller Boris Klinsky was a perspiring, pallid, fearful man who never talked above a droning whisper made more incomprehensible by a thick accent. Preston's elation at finishing the dreary job was muted by a headache. The scrap of paper in his pocket with the phone number of Miss Dottie Farrel, the cute blonde who'd been his first interviewee, had been forgotten.

"Noah, I do feel a bit used up. Perhaps lunch will lift me up."

Pflam donned his cap and saluted. "Yes sir, I know just the thing to raise your spirits. Have those peckish mornings myself occasionally."

In the car Pflam's directions took them from the business district north through residential neighborhoods toward the docks. Preston slowed the car as it descended the steeply sloping street past warehouses where workmen were unloading trucks. Near where the wharfs met the railroad tracks Pflam called a halt.

Across the cobbled street a small group of men in ragged garb were resting against large wooden handcarts filled with trash. "Rag pickers," Pflam nodded toward the group. "A cardboard box or a bit of cloth is a fortune to those poor devils."

As they exited the Ford, a nearby railroad ferry sounded a horn as it edged toward the dock. Screeching gulls rose into the midday sky. Outside the car there were the heavy odors of oil, polluted water and rotting wood. At the doors to a large two-story wooden building his assistant waited for him.

Preston looked up at the wooden sign painted by some amateur artist. Beneath a smirking dancing woman of improbable dimensions black letters spelled out Hardy's Tavern. The front of the wooden building had once been painted gray but patches of the paint had peeled away to reveal dark boards.

"Looks a bit rough, I know. But it is a fine place for a sandwich and a beer."

Inside the building a crowd of twenty or so men stood about. Preston knew that these were the men "on the scratch." They had run out of money before they had gotten drunk. Now they stood about waiting for an opportunity to scratch up some money. The men stood aside to let Pflam and Preston enter. But their scarred faces showed their animosity.

Pflam paid no attention to the menacing looks but called out in a cheery voice, "Halloo there, my boys. Andy, Tony, Rocco, how you doing? Paddy, out already? Thought you had another few months." The men nodded in response.

The two policemen entered a barn-like room that took up the entire first floor of the building. On the left a bar with a brass rail extended to the rear wall. Two perspiring bartenders stopped their work to watch the newcomers.

On the right there were round wooden tables with mismatched chairs. Though it was midday customers stood three deep at the bar. The tables were occupied and the din was almost paralyzing.

"Upstairs, sir," Pflam shouted, "is where the more social-minded ladies take their gentlemen friends for a visit."

Waitresses toting large round trays held over their heads hurried through the crowd to deliver drinks and sandwiches.

Pflam stopped at a table occupied by a group of men. "Ah, a meeting of the Sunday School board of governors, is it?" Pflam shouted to be heard above the din. "Pete, Shiv, Barney, why don't you boys get some exercise? Take a walk, my friend and I need to have a private conversation."

Slowly the men, muttering, rose and left. The policemen sat down.

"Noah, haven't seen you in a while." A young waitress wearing a full skirt and revealing peasant blouse stood close to the seated policeman. Her lipstick was smeared and she gave Preston an unsteady sidelong look.

"Rita, my little pansy," Pflam slid a hand round her waist. "I know it's difficult but we are, so to speak, on duty so no fraternizing.

She bowed her head, smiling. "Sorry, sir. Officer Pflam, the usual?"

He coughed and stole a look at his boss. "Me and the gentle-man will have schooners and your best beef sandwiches." He sent her on her way with a pat.

Pflam unbuttoned his jacket and slouched in the chair. "In a moment you'll be right as rain." Lighting a cigarette he took a long meditative drag. "I like to come here, hobnob with the criminal element, so to speak. Helps to keep in touch. Identify illegalities before they are perpetrated."

Preston nodded but did not feel like talking. His headache was not being helped by the noise and the odors.

Rita returned with the two sandwiches and two huge schooners of dark beer.

Preston took a sip from the beer. It took an effort for him to swallow. The stuff was swill. Pflam had taken a big drink and bit into the sandwich.

"Rita," Preston got her attention. "Bring me a double shot of Four Roses and a glass of water, please." She hurried off again. "Here, Pflam, you drink this. I don't drink beer very often," he lied.

"Thank you very much. I will take care of this orphan." As he chewed, he slid his empty mug to the edge of the table and took hold of the full one. "I don't drink much of the hard liquor. Daresay it is more a gentleman's drink, beer is good enough for the likes of myself."

Preston drank his whiskey and took a sip of water. He felt better. The sandwich was quite good.

"Officer Noah Pflam," a stocky man wearing a cloth cap pulled down to his eyes and a flannel shirt several sizes too big with the collar pulled up to his chin, sat down at the table. As he leaned forward Preston saw that a scar running from eye to mouth puckered the right side of his face. "Please, you got a buck for me?"

Pflam chewed slowly, swallowed and then looked at the interloper. "Flip Delanty ain't it? And didn't I just hear that you were enjoying the hospitality of the state?"

"A mistake Officer Pflam. Innocent. A smash-and-grab charge. You know that ain't my style."

Pflam scowled, "Style? When did the likes of you have a style?"

Delanty moved closer to the table. "Didn't mean nothing. You know I ain't a heavy one, a rough guy. That lockup put me in a real bad place. Give me a little help, sir. I need some green."

Pflam had finished his lunch and his beer. He looked about for Rita. "Sorry for your troubles, Flip. But we only pay for the real goods: names, addresses."

Delanty took a cigarette butt from his pocket and lit it with a match. As he smoked he looked about nervously and whispered.

Pflam responded sharply, "Have to speak up. Can't read your lips."

"I heard about some car snatching going on. Some real hard cases. Strangers from Detroit."

The officer sat up and sneered. "Rumors are hot air. You think we been born yesterday? Get out of here."

Preston touched Pflam's arm and slid two dollars bills onto the table.

"You're in luck. My superior is a tender hearted man, Flip." As Delanty reached for the money the officer's hand closed over his. "But my thieving friend you owe us. Bring us names and locations. Soon."

Chapter 15

Friday and a quiet cup of coffee alone in the kitchen, Dorothea cherished these moments. She loved the morning rush, serving breakfast, making sure her roomers were sent well fed to their day. The time alone was her reward after the work. Now, dishes washed and dried, kitchen shining, sitting and sipping a hot drink she let her mind wander. Later she'd do the planning for her day.

Maybe this weekend would be when Preston invited her to walk on the beach. Since that first morning it seemed the poor fellow hadn't had time to stroll anywhere. He'd been busy running around Grand Haven with that rascal Noah Pflam. Though Pflam didn't have a very good reputation, he wasn't a bad sort really. Smiling and shaking her head Dorothea was reminded that there were connections in this life that she would never understand. And what other women saw in Noah was one of those imponderables. The man had three families she knew of. The guy was pudgy, not very good looking and drank beer all the time, though that little moustache was kind of cute.

Preston didn't have a mustache, but he was good looking in a mature, almost moody way. She'd always been drawn to fellows with dark, deep eyes. Seemed they were always thinking, trying to figure out life. Philippe had been like that. Dorothea's automatic warning signal went off. Careful girl! Every time she got to thinking about a guy's dreamy eyes she ended up falling for him. After that it was too late. Careful? She'd be careful. They might walk on the beach that was all.

Taking care of her roomers kept her busy and she loved running the boarding house but there was still the loneliness in the night. She put her cup in the sink and glanced at her face in the mirror. Not bad looking. Mary Fulton had told her she looked like a movie star. Well, maybe not quite that good but pretty enough for a walk, maybe hold hands a bit.

"Yewhoo, are you busy?" Dorothea looked through the window over the sink into the back yard. There near the clothesline her neighbor, Opal Meacham was waving to invite her out for a chat over the fence. Dorothea waved back, got out a large mug and filled it with coffee. Two teaspoons of sugar and lots of milk just the way Opal liked it, then she went down the back stairs to the yard.

"Thought you might be too busy for a visit this morning," Opal greeted her.

"Always work to do, but never so much that a bit of a chat can't be fit in." She handed the mug to Opal. Then she pushed against the old wooden fence that separated their properties. "Why don't we tear this splintery old thing down, Opal? I'll get some lawn chairs and a table, then we can sit and visit in comfort."

"That'd be nice but who's got money for work like that?" The fence creaked as the neighbor leaned against it. Opal was wide-bodied, heavy and she had a job, poor thing, that kept her on her feet all day.

"Guess you're right." Her friend's job paid little and money was a common and painful topic for her. "Opal, what are you doing home? Thought the hospital had you on the day shift?"

She rested the mug on the top rail after she had drunk and shook her head so vigorously that her chins vibrated. "Hospitals take care of folks, supposed to anyway. They sure don't take care of the people working for them. Hospital told me I had to work a split shift. Got to go in at noon til three and then back at six to clean up after supper. I swear my hands are going to grow to that mop." She stopped, eyes moist, to take another drink of coffee. "Six days a week, twelve hours a day..."

"Why Opal that's slavery."

"You're telling me? But what can I do? When Jimmie got killed I had to go to work. It's the only way I can hang onto the house."

"You got nothing from the construction company Jimmie worked for when that wall fell on him?"

"Not a penny. One day we were getting by all right and had the house, and the next I was struggling to keep the house and stay off the streets. When I got this job at the General Hospital I thought it was a gift from heaven. Now..." She shrugged her shoulders and emptied the mug.

Dorothea fell silent. With all her rooms rented, the work had multiplied. She had considered getting a girl in to help her. But she didn't think Opal could handle the work and the stairs.

She handed Dorothea the empty mug. "Sure was good coffee. I suppose I shouldn't drink it. I have been having trouble sleeping. Wake up in the middle of the night, lay there worrying." Her neighbor lost her battle with tears. She wiped the moisture away with her hand. "Now I've got other things worrying me something terrible."

Dorothea knew that her friend could not be hurried into telling what was really bothering her. She remained silent while Opal took a deep breath preparing herself for the news. "That sister I got, Ruby, lives in Detroit, remember I told you about her?"

"Sure, I remember. Ruby lost her husband last year. How is she doing, her and the kids?"

"She had it rough, real tough for a while. She took care of Bennie when his kidneys went bad. Big strong fellow just melted away, died, and then she got herself married again." She swiped at her eyes again and looked out at the lake. Dorothea wondered why Opal seemed so downcast. Marriage would seem to have solved Ruby's problems.

"Ruby didn't marry no laborer. He's got his own truck and delivers stuff in Detroit."

"Well, he'll be a good provider then. Does he get along with Ruby's kids?"

"She had such a terrible time keeping the family together. Welfare was going to take all three kids and put them in a home." The tears were coming again. "I tried to help her as much as I could."

"But things should be getting better for Ruby, right?"

"Yeah, sort of," she agreed grudgingly. "But Earl, that's her new husband, Earl Duffy, is kind of funny. Oh, he gets along all right with the two younger ones, the boys."

Opal stopped to take a breath and wipe her face again.

"Ruby's oldest," she whispered and averted her eyes, "is Emma, she ain't but thirteen but almost a woman already. According to Ruby Earl is taking a real strong interest in her." When she looked at her friend Opal's pain was clear. "You know what I mean?"

Dorothea's gasp of denial was a reflex. She held the fence and nodded.

"Like I said, Earl provides for everyone, is real good with the boys, but Ruby is scared for Emma. She wants to get her away from him. Wants to send the child here to me. She got it all figured out and told me in a letter. Ruby'd tell Earl Emma's coming here to learn hospital work." Opal smoothed the front of her dowdy dress and looked over her shoulder at her small house. "I could clear out the box room and put a bed in it. But the hospital ain't hiring now and, if there's no job, I don't see how I could feed her. Dorothea I just get by on the little bit I make."

It took a moment for Dorothea to make sure her voice was steady. The words came out slowly.

"Opal, you give Ruby a call. Come use my phone right now. You tell Ruby that if she'll get Emma over here I'll give her a job. It'll be a temporary one and I can't pay much." Even with six roomers, hiring a helper would tighten the budget.

"Oh, my goodness, a long-distance call?" Dorothea waved away her concern. What difference was the cost? A child's life was at sake.

"Bless you Dorothea Dugan. Bless you, you got a good heart." Opal reached across the fence and held her left hand tightly.

Dorothea sniffed, "I could use help with the cleaning."

Opal was back in her house getting some rest before she had to go to work. The call to Detroit had been made. Dorothea had heard the mother's sounds of joy and relief. The girl would arrive on the train in a week or so.

No accounting for humans, Dorothea thought again. Making a little money, saving a bit even, and she had to hire someone. The help would be appreciated. But if circumstances had allowed her to wait a little longer she might have saved enough money to get the front of the house painted.

She turned on the light and sat at the small table in the kitchen. Deftly she used the small boning knife to pick out the splinters she'd driven into her hand when Opal told her about Emma.

She had to help. It was her nature. Standing at the sink, letting the cold water run over her right hand to sooth the splinter wounds and wash the blood away the image of the hovel where she first saw the light of day came to her. In the Indiana hamlet it had been the older, almost grown up Bolton brothers who had introduced her to fear and pain. It mustn't happen to Emma.

Chapter 16

The right front tire of the Ford rode up onto the curb and bumped back down onto the street. The error in steering surprised Preston; he'd thought he was parking quite smoothly. His mistake was excusable; it had been a long, tiring day and there had been a couple of drinks with Pflam at Hardy's, that dreadful tavern. Later at the police station when he'd finished writing the report, Milton Spivak had shown up and gotten his bottle out. He closed his eyes and rested his head on the steering wheel. In a moment, once he'd rested and gathered himself, he'd go in to Dorothea's house. He needed to get to bed.

Dorothea listened for a moment to the post dinner music provided by Minnie Quinton. She played her rendition of "Thanks for the Memory", a popular tune from a recent movie. Dorothea moved to the front door to check that the outside light was on. She heard a thump and looked out.

There was a dark sedan in front of the house, and for a moment Dorothea did not recognize it. The figure slumped against the steering wheel looked like Preston and she wondered if she should go out to see if he was feeling ill. No, it might not be Preston and what would she say to a stranger? The figure in the car sat up. It was Preston and Dorothea felt a small thrill as she watched him get out, pocket the keys and start up the stairs. She hurried into the front room where she pretended to listen to the music. Preston entered the house. His uneven, limping steps led him to her side.

"Detective, you're back." Her feigned surprise sounded mannered and false but she couldn't take back her words. The hollows beneath his eyes were dark, the lines round them deeper. The poor man must have had a difficult day. "You must be worn out and hungry. Come to the kitchen and I'll get you something to eat."

Preston nodded and followed her slowly.

Behind them Mordechai leaned over to say something to Beryl Richards while Minnie looked through the sheet music for another song. Accompanied by Clement, Nils had gone out to find out if he might send a telegram from the Western Union office to his sister-in-law in Europe.

The kitchen retained the warmth from the just completed meal. Looking around Preston protested, "You've just tidied up. There's no need for you to mess things up."

"Preston, a sandwich and a drink will not mess the kitchen. It's no trouble at all." She hurried about the room getting a plate and utensils.

"Please sit down. Relax, it won't take me a minute."

He obediently sat and observed her.

"Water or would you like for me to brew some coffee?"

"Water will be fine. And thank you very much, Dorothea."

She stopped rummaging in the refrigerator and turned to him holding a package wrapped in white butcher paper. "You are certainly welcome."

Crackling butcher paper was folded back, "Would you like

the ham for your sandwich warmed?"

"Oh, no, cold will be just fine."

She opened the refrigerator and leaned over to peer in to it. "Mayonnaise or mustard or both?"

"Mustard I think."

Opening the breadbox she announced, "I have white, wheat or rye bread."

"My what a feast in a sandwich. I'd like some rye please."

With a flourish she set the plate with the sandwich on the table in front of him and placed a napkin next to it.

After replacing the bread in the box Dorothea moved toward the door. Preston asked, "Won't you sit with me?"

She stopped and moved to the table to sit opposite him. "I thought that after a long day you'd enjoy the quiet."

"Not at all. I'd enjoy talking with you."

"Well, okay, if you want me to."

"It is a relief that all that interviewing and gathering information is over. Pflam, poor fellow, slept in the chair next to the typist. She was hammering away while he snored." He chuckled at the memory. "I'd have liked to join him but I had my final report on that bank robbery to write. It's all done now. Tomorrow afternoon the interviews and the whole thing will be in the hands of Detective Anderson, my boss." He took a long drink. "Then Sergeant Spivak wants me to help look into a matter concerning stolen autos."

"I hope you'll have some time to rest." Taking a pitcher of ice water from the refrigerator she refilled his glass. "I expect you must get tired of asking people questions all day long."

"It can get tedious. People would be surprised how much of police work involves passive things – waiting and listening."

"And most people think being a policeman involves chases, shoot-outs and, well, dangers. You know, hoodlums with guns and that sort of thing."

He looked down at his thigh and rubbed his aching hip. "There's some of that. But fortunately it's rare. But you are right. When people hear that I'm a cop they want to hear about the chases, gun play and the famous criminals I've met." He took a bite of the sandwich and chewed. "That's very good, Dorothea." He took a long drink. "Just what the doctor ordered."

"Thank you, Preston. What you said before about people's interest in the imagined excitement of your work. I'm probably being foolish but I'd think the contact with the people would be most interesting in an investigation. Figuring out motives and why people do what they do."

"Not foolish at all." He wiped his hands and mouth and placed the napkin on the empty plate. Then he drained his glass. "I agree with your assessment. Went right to the complex and challenging part of this work." He laughed and his sound was gruff, even sarcastic. "Humans are an infinitely confusing tribe, aren't we? Frustrating and, forgive my language, damnable and self-damning."

As she cleared the table she thought about his words. At the sink, her back to him, she asked softly. "You think we are weak and selfish creatures?"

"To tell the truth, Dorothea, right now I am not sure what I really think."

They listened as Minnie played something slow and very pretty.

"Very nice," he said.

"I think it is Chopin, an e'tude," she replied.

The wavering, declining Doppler notes of a ship's horn filled the kitchen for a moment drowning out the music.

"I hope I'm not being too forward." He stood up slowly. "Let's take a walk along the shore."

"But you were favoring your leg, limping. Ought you?" She gestured towards his hip.

"Just a short walk. It is such a fine evening. A bit of exercise will help digestion." He held out a hand. "Come on, please."

Dorothea took off her apron and hurried to get her sweater.

❧ ❧ ❧

They had to control their rapid breathing and inclination to laugh out loud when they returned from their tramp. Fueled by a sudden happiness Dorothea'd run the last hundred yards or so uphill to the house. Walking slowly, Preston had followed.

While she caught her breath on the porch he followed her and got out his key. He opened the door and allowed Dorothea to enter first.

"Oh, my" she gasped as she unbuttoned her coat. "Running around like a schoolgirl. I'm glad it's dark, someone might have seen me."

"I'm sure any observers would have admired your agility. You won the competition easily." Preston was short of breath but he felt great.

In the front hallway with the door locked they shared looks for a moment in the dim light. He reached out and touched her arm. Dorothea said his name.

Preston lifted her arm, held her hand and kissed it gently. She patted his cheek and watched as he made his halting way up the stairs before she turned off the lights.

Chapter 17

The next morning as the roomers ate breakfast, the quiet was interrupted by Preston's question. "Dorothea, what is your favorite song?"

She knew that he was teasing her in front of the roomers. Earlier, while she'd been preparing the meal, Preston had snuck into the kitchen and kissed her hand again.

Now, as she ate she had been deep in reverie, but his question jerked her back to reality. Everyone was looking at her. She successfully repressed the nervous laugh that struggled to erupt.

"I'm sure that one of the songs by Mister Irving Berlin would be my favorite. Perhaps "What'll I Do?" That would certainly be among the songs I love most."

"What is the first line? I can't seem to recall."

Dorothea recited the first lines from memory.

> What'll I do
>
> When you are far away
>
> And I am blue
>
> What'll I do?

He smiled impishly. "Indeed, that is a fine song. I find his "Always" a lovely song too. Do you recall the first line? I declare my memory is still asleep."

Dorothea did indeed remember the opening line. She recited them quietly in her mind: "I'll be loving you always/ with a love that's true always." But Preston's tactic to get her to say she loved him in front of everyone would not work.

"I confess that I do not. Can you refresh my memory?" She fibbed.

He shook his head. His face was a pleasant shade of pink. "I can't. It's a shame. I would like very much to hear you sing."

"Your detecting fails you this time. Were I to sing, I might very well ruin everyone's meal."

Everyone laughed and Preston saluted Dorothea with his table knife.

"Here, here, I got one," Dorothea was pleased to see the brightening of Nils' mood since his successful trip to the Western Union store to send a telegram to Denmark. Now he offered to perform a ditty he'd learned as a young Great Lakes sailor. In a gruff but merry voice he sang about seamen having girls in every port. He finished the English version and sang it again in his native Danish. No one understood the second version but somehow the lyrics seemed more risqué than the first version.

Minnie Quinton assisted the musical recital by keeping time tapping her knife on the table. To everyone's surprise Preston rose and bowed, "I trust that no one will be shocked by my song. It was introduced by Groucho Marx in the film "A Day at the Circus." In a pleasant tenor voice he sang of the beauties of "Lydia the Tattooed Lady."

Minnie and Beryl tittered behind hands covering their mouths. Though she enjoyed Preston's rendition, Dorothea felt her cheeks warm as she listened to his voice. She looked straight ahead and would not give Preston a chance to smirk at her.

Preston was the star of the morning. The enthusiastic ovation he received brought the singing to an end.

Reluctantly the group broke up. Mordechai bowed to Preston and announced to Dorothea he would take his morning walk. Misses Richards and Quinton planned a trip to the library, then a visit to the haberdashers. As Nils got ready to leave he explained to Dorothea that his companion Clement was not feeling well. This morning Nils would have to stroll alone down to the docks and watch the ships loading.

Preston stayed behind to help Dorothea collect the dishes. She went ahead into the kitchen and filled the sink with hot soapy water. She hoped he'd follow but she still jumped a little when he touched her back.

"I must go to the police station to talk to Sergeant Spivak about some stolen vehicles. Don't know when I'll be back." He took hold of her arm and turned her so that she faced him.

"Careful," she protested, "My hands are all soapy. I'll get your shirt wet. Milton will think you swam there."

Smiling he let go and stepped back. "OK, Dorothea. But one question before I leave."

"Yes, what is it?"

"Will you walk with me again?"

She did not trust her voice, so she nodded. Afraid that he hadn't seen the motion, she said, "Of course."

He touched her arm and then was gone.

Her hands were deep in the hot water when she remembered what Nils had told her. Clement was sick again. Poor man.

≈ ≈ ≈

She tapped at the door to Clement's room. There was no response. Balancing the tray on her left hand she turned the doorknob with her right. The door swung open.

The shade was pulled down, the room was dark; it took a moment for Dorothea's eyes to adjust. The bed was mussed but empty. Clothed in the shirt and trousers he'd worn yesterday, the old man was slumped in a chair next to the bed.

Window shut tight, the room smelled of perspiration and unwashed clothes. She put the tray holding the coffee and toast on the bed and looked more closely at Clement. His eyes were closed and his skin had a bluish pallor. She watched for a moment and her heart sank. She had allowed Clement to die all alone. There had been no one to talk to him, to hold his hand and ease his passage. Controlling her angry frustration, Dorothea touched his shoulder. Clement inhaled painfully, groaned and arched his back. He was alive though he was in pain.

Had the poor man sat in the chair all night? That wasn't right. She must make him more comfortable. Dorothea hurried down the hall to the washroom and wet a cloth. Returning, she gently bathed his face, calling his name. His eyelids fluttered.

Clement tried to raise his right arm but let it fall back to his lap. His eyes opened and focused on her. "Oh, Dorothea, my arm, chest, hurt. Help me."

Poor man, his suffering must end.

She whispered in his ear. "I'm going to help you to my room. I've got an easy chair you can rest in. There'll be a cool breeze from the window. I'll get you a nice drink. Got some gin."

He smacked his bluish lips. "Thank you. But I'm not feeling real chipper."

"We'll do it together."

      ❧   ❧   ❧

The one flight of stairs up to her room was not as difficult to climb as Dorothea thought it would be. The old man was tough and she was sturdy. He was resting now in her chair. He'd drunk some gin and told her he felt better. He was sleeping.

She took the glass from his limp fingers and put it on the table. While he slept, she'd get things ready.

On a step stool, standing on her tiptoes, she reached the back of the highest cabinet above the sink. The black leather case given her by Nate Malan was there. She held it while she folded the stool. Then she carefully dusted off the case. It was about the size of a hardbound book and she hadn't touched it in a while.

Leaning against the sink, Dorothea stared past Clement to the gray lake now whipped into white caps by the wind. This was not easy but it was the right thing to do.

The sound of Clement's labored breathing roused her. Every time she got the case down she had this argument with herself. The sound of the case being unzipped was the only other sound in the room.

❧   ❧   ❧

Several years ago back in Hollywood when she'd met Nate and agreed to care for him. He was dying. He had a lung disease that had left him so weak that he could barely make it to the toilet and back to the bed where he spent his days.

When he decided to return to Michigan to die, Dorothea drove his Buick. They traveled for as long as Nate could stand it and then she found a motor court and rented a room. Once he was in bed he regaled her with stories of his days as an almost successful screenwriter.

He told her of the story he wrote and nearly sold to a big studio about an evil scientist who got rid of rivals by poisoning them with nicotine.

"Everybody smokes so there's some nicotine in us all. And it's a deadly poison," he'd explain as he waved his ever-present cigarette in the air. "Cops couldn't catch him. It was a sure hit. Could have been a Sherlock Holmes or Boston Blackie feature film."

"I got the plot worked out. Had Chester Morris, the guy who played Boston Blackie, chasing the evil Doctor Schwartz all over the place. It was a real thriller, a sure hit." Nate stopped to light a cigarette and finish a coughing fit. "Suddenly the studio wasn't interested. Found out later that the marketing director of a big tobacco company had visited. And my story was in the waste basket."

He'd researched the story thoroughly. When he got excited telling her about the script, he had her get out the black case that held his painkiller medicine. From among the pills he had her take out the small vial that held purified nicotine so she could see how little it took.

"Sweetheart, don't ever get these mixed up with the morphine." He'd make a breathless sound that was his laugh.

He'd taught Dorothea how to inject him with the painkillers, he needed more often as the disease progressed. When the painkillers no longer worked, Nate had shown her how to inject him with the nicotine. He hadn't suffered, he had been a good teacher. When he died near Grand Haven she had kept the case.

❧   ❧   ❧

In a few minutes she'd wake Clement. They'd talk about Polly, his wife, and how much he missed her. After another drink or two of gin she was sure the old man would drowse once more, maybe even sleep. Then she'd take out a hypodermic and fill it with the right amount of nicotine she'd purified from garden pesticide.

As the drug spread out in him Clement might wake and feel sick for a moment. That wasn't very likely. His weakened heart would likely just stop beating; his passing would be peaceful.

The familiar sorrow filled her. Even the grief was a necessary feeling. He mustn't suffer anymore.

She was doing her duty. It was what she must do.

Chapter 18

"You have family?" Milton Spivak enquired. Preston knew that Spivak was just being friendly. He had no idea that Preston had a difficult time talking about his marriage. He and Preston were walking around downtown Lake Harbor. The main traffic to the docks and railroad yard followed a path two blocks west so while they heard the racket, the streets they walked had little traffic.

Preston dropped behind as he answered. First he breathed deeply and made himself relax. "Divorced. Got a daughter. She lives in New Hampshire with her mother."

"That's tough. You don't get to see her much?" Spivak noticed that Preston had dropped behind and was limping. "Sorry, Preston. I get out of that office and I guess I just want to run a foot race." He slowed his rapid gait and walked beside his companion. "Your limp, a gift from Killer Kelly?"

Preston nodded and stopped to light a cigarette. Spivak remained at his side. "That was a real job you did on that maniac."

Preston shrugged. There was nothing to be said. He did not remember much about the shootout. He'd been drinking steadily for a week. This morning he had the familiar sharp headache, the result of the celebration last night after sending off to Anderson the bank robbery report.

"Real brave that was," Spivak said. After glancing up at Preston he changed his tone. "Well, all settled in at Dorothea's?"

He smiled and nodded. "She takes good care of us. A great cook." They stopped to allow a Ford Club Coupe to pass. "Haven't had much opportunity to enjoy her hospitality. The last few days I've been busy interviewing witnesses to the bank robbery, getting the testimony typed up. I don't believe we'll be bothered by this foolishness anymore."

The police sergeant waved his hand in the air as if brushing away mosquitoes. "No offence, but that is a waste of taxpayers money, isn't it? The FBI guy, Hoover, got his fingers in that pie, didn't he?"

"Yeah, he did."

"Had trouble finding all the witnesses, did you?"

"Some of the customers might have been more difficult if Officer Pflam hadn't been around to help.. He knows this town inside and out."

"I thought he'd be of some help. Pflam's not a bad sort really if you forgive his weakness for the ladies and beer. He usually finds both the beer and the ladies at Hardy's Tavern. Did he ever take you to that dive?"

"Indeed, he did. And, I think, he may have gotten us a lead on the stolen cars."

Spivak stopped and a look of joyful surprise lit up his narrow face. "Tell me about it."

"Could be. You mentioned Hardy's and that reminded me of an incident that took place there."

"I'm waiting."

"Do you know a hoodlum named Flip Delanty?"

Spivak nodded, "I not only know the devil, I've dragged him in to a cell more than once. A real plug-ugly that one, lowest of the low."

"Yes, I got that impression. He wanted some money, been in the slammer and was hard up. Wanted some money, but Pflam wouldn't come across. So Flip gave us what he had. He told us he'd heard of a gang, new to the neighborhood, that's snatching cars and selling them to bank robbers."

"No."

"Yeah, and this gang is ramrodded by an old safe cracker. I gave Delanty a couple of bucks and sent him off to get more information."

Spivak grabbed Preston's jacket sleeve and hurriedly turned him around. "That's it, my boy. Let's get back to my office. I want to call your boss, Anderson is it? After I get you loose and working with us, we can get out in the county and look for these thieves."

"You go on ahead, don't wait for me. Let's get this posse organized."

      ح   ح   ح

Spivak set the phone back into the black cradle and exhaled with relief. "Your boss is not an easy man, is he?" Preston smiled but did not speak.

Spivak took up the phone again. "I'll call the sheriff and see if I can't get some help. We need to get some units out on the dirt roads looking for the car thieves."

"Just a minute, Spivak, hear me out." He set the phone down and waited for Preston to have his say. "I did a lot of undercover work with the state police. People trust my face, I guess, and I'm a born liar. Can make up a story that most people believe."

"Even the crooks?"

"Yep, especially them. If that retired safe cracker was a ripper who tore the backs off safes with a crowbar, then he'll be a burly fellow. The gang will need a place they can live and it has to be close to a barn where they hide the stolen cars. This narrows the search some."

"Yeah, Preston, I see what you are going for here. But there'll be several gangsters and they will be on the lookout. And this is a big county."

"OK, but let me finish. The hideout has to be near a paved road so they can deliver the goods quickly. It wouldn't do for them to have a stolen Packard stuck in the mud. I'll bet there aren't many paved roads going south toward Illinois and Indiana, are there?" Preston slowly lit a cigarette while Milton was deep in thought.

The sergeant looked up at the detective and a slow smile creased his face. Preston smiled back, "You know it will work. I'll drive around the old dirt roads like some lost city slicker. At this stage it will be best for me to do this alone. Less likely for our cover to get blown." The cloud of tobacco smoke Preston exhaled rose slowly. He leaned forward and ground out the cigarette. "Trust me, I'll have a story that will keep those robbers relaxed. When I spot them, I'll come back here and then we can get some officers from the sheriff. Those thieves will never know what hit them."

Spivak nodded and opened the lower drawer of his desk.

"And it will be case closed." He poured large drinks and pushed one toward Preston. "I'll put Pflam back on the streets and have him keep an eye on Delanty. Get any new information and I'll pass it on to you. Yeah, it will work." Smiling, they clicked their glasses and drank. Spivak set his empty glass down with a thump. "Damn, catching the bad guys, punishing them, that's what it is all about, right?" Preston swallowed a gulp of whiskey and nodded slowly.

Chapter 19

Dorothea's spirit was at peace now. Though the relief she'd given Clement had not been easy on her it had been right. Now she would handle the aftermath. While all the roomers were out the mortician's black limousine had come and picked up his remains. Clement would be handled fittingly. His stone would bear the name of a person who died long ago in another place. She'd been careful so things would go no further. A question or two might be asked but then life would move on.

Now the hardest part was hiding her grief. Sorrow was a physical weight in her mind. Moving, doing everyday things required effort as if her limbs were buried in sand. She'd retreat into her self and there deal with the loss of a friend. Grief could be put in a private place and dealt with there. It could be done; she'd done it before. Now it was important that she go through the motions; act as if nothing had changed. Appearance would be everything.

∾ ∾ ∾

Dorothea prepared a meal of gravy from pot roast scraps and boiled potatoes. A small treat for her charges. As she worked in the kitchen she heard her guests returning from their days. Beryl and Minnie chatted merrily as they went upstairs to get ready for supper. Carefully closing the door, Mordechai stepped lightly as he hurried to his room as if he were apologizing for any sound he made. Nils stumbled on the stairs. He'd probably been drinking beer with his cronies. She listened for Preston but he did not come. She set the meal on the table and called for everyone to come down.

Dorothea made sure that all were eating before she sat down to her own meal. She sliced her boiled potato and took a small bite. Breathing deeply she chewed slowly, carefully. She smiled round at the roomers and hoped no one would want to talk.

"Evening everyone, sorry I'm late. Lost track of the time."

Preston's deep voice surprised Dorothea and drew her out of her thoughts.

"I think everything's still warm. Just help yourself, Preston," Dorothea greeted him.

He eagerly pulled out a chair and sat down. Minnie handed him the plate of potatoes while Beryl made sure he had some gravy. Mordechai greeted Preston and inquired about his day. Nils nodded and filled his mouth again.

"I trust you've had a profitable and eventful day Mister Duhamel."

"Mister McNeil, I have had a very constructive day talking with a friend. Then I drove to the edge of Lake Harbor, on the east and walked around a bit."

"Oh," Mordechai McNeil protested with a shiver, "that was brave. I've heard that those abandoned buildings out there are simply crawling with vermin, snakes perhaps. Vagrants and even gypsies are living in some of the old farmhouses."

"Perhaps so," Preston replied. "Yet I saw no one or any thing. The worst I have to report is a little tiredness and some sand in my shoes."

"We're happy you returned safely." Beryl said and then blushed.

"Dorothea, this is excellent." He grinned at her saluting with his fork. She mumbled a response, lowered her gaze and concentrated on her plate.

Nils finished eating and went into the front room where he found a comfortable seat on the sofa and fell asleep. Mordechai McNeil and the two women followed. His hands rested on their shoulders as he spoke softly to them. Minnie sat at the piano and softly played "Maybe", a tune recently popularized by Bing Crosby.

"May I help you clean up, Dorothea?" Preston asked.

"Aren't you tired from your expedition?"

"No, I dumped the sand out of my shoes and had a fine meal. I feel absolutely frisky."

Without responding she rose from the table and began to collect the supper things. There was no protest from her when he stacked the dishes on his side of the table. In the kitchen he rinsed the plates while she filled the sink with hot water and added Lux flakes. Without speaking she took the china stacked by Preston and submerged them. The repetitive motion involved in washing the plates and dipping them in the rinse water took all her attention. As Preston dried them and stacked the clean plates on the table he tried to engage Dorothea in conversation. When she did not respond he stopped his work and look at her quizzically.

"Are you all right?" Preston asked the question softly. He was afraid that he might have done something to upset her.

Before she could respond Nils bumbled into the kitchen and stood there, as if shocked to find himself awake and in the kitchen. Dorothea dried her hands, turned and faced the old man.

"Scuse." Nils apologized. "Don't mean to interrupt nor nothing." The old man stuttered as he searched for the words to convey what he came to say.

"That's fine, Nils. How can I help you?" Despite the encouragement the old man remained mute, gazing from one to the other.

"Nils, you interrupted nothing. Preston is simply helping me wash the dishes. What is it you want?" Dorothea asked tensely.

The old man did not look up from the floor as he spoke. "Well, thought I might go up and look in on Clement. See how he is. Wanted to find out from you, Dorothea, if you thought that would be a good idea. Don't want to wake him up or make him feel worse, you know."

"How nice of you, Nils. But that won't be necessary. His family came by this afternoon and picked him up. Silas, a younger brother, and his son, Jeffrey, Clement's nephew, came for him. They had a nice, big car. They were going to take him to a sanitarium where he will be cared for quite well."

The old sailor looked stunned. "Never got a chance to say goodbye. Didn't know he had any family, never mentioned any. Did they leave an address?"

"Jeffrey said he'd send us one soon. Clement knew we cared, all of us. Told me to tell you that you were a good friend. He'll be more comfortable now. Be happy for him, Nils, he has such a good family."

With Nils, Preston was surprised at the abrupt departure, but he was happy that Clement was with his family. He patted Nils on the back as the old man left the kitchen shaking his head and murmuring "We were friends."

Dorothea dabbed her eyes and went back to the dishes. "I'll miss him, even the fusses he had with Nils." The words helped keep at bay the sadness that threatened to overcome her. Preston agreed as he stacked the clean dishes. Dorothea made a small sound of frustration and anger then took up a wet cloth to wipe the worktable and stove.

He took the cloth from Dorothea gently and held her hand.

"Dorothea," he said softly, "You're going to polish the shine off that stove." She smiled at him and folded her hands.

"Let's take a short stroll along the lakeshore, look at the lights and then we'll call it a night."

"Yes," she replied, "call it a night."

They walked to the beacon and sat in the sand by the jetty. Overhead the range lights that helped ships to safely find the harbor circled through the dark.

Dorothea ran her hand over her eyes and looked out into the dark above the lake. "Life's about adapting isn't it? Learning to get along with things changing?"

"Yes," he replied. "I think it is." He held up a handful of sand and let it seep between his fingers. "I think I know how you are feeling. They transfer us about a lot. Whenever I am reassigned I feel upset. I don't know. It's a sense of loss."

"Loss. That's the right word." She said the word again.

"Loss."

"It'll be fine." He took her hand.

"Fine. Yes, fine."

"You look tired." He gently touched her hair. The distant illumination highlighted the fine planes of her face.

Preston kissed and embraced her. She rested her face against his chest.

"I'm lonely." She whispered. There were several moments of silence before she spoke again. "Preston, I don't want to be alone tonight. Do you understand?"

Preston stroked her hair and then answered. "Yes, dear, I do."

Chapter 20

Jerked from sleep by the chilled pawing of fear, Preston was rigid as his mind unreeled shame. He was a total failure; his career as a detective was over. He wasn't loved and couldn't love. The inchoate fear filled his mind; it turned and scratched inside his skull. Leg muscles tautened to flee the dream threat spasmed into a cramp. Fully awake he strove to relax and to ease the pain. The room was cold and he'd kicked the blankets into a tangle. Sitting up he straightened out the covers, covered his head with them and fell back again into a protective ball.

As his body warmed, the taut hip slowly relaxed. The moonlight through the small window opposite his bed shone on a silvery, indistinct scene. If he concentrated, he could make out the dark outlines of the roof peaks of the houses on the hillside below. He closed his eyes and breathed slowly. A dog barked and the continual susurrus of the lake waves lulled him.

"You wake up at night and you be sweating like a pig." Walt warned him at the treatment center. "No reason for it. Maybe you had a good day, maybe not. But the panic and the night-sweats come. Your body is fighting your brain. Your body is telling you to get it a drink of alcohol, your head is warning you to stay away from the booze."

Walt told him that alcohol was cunning and insidious. Whiskey would lurk in Preston's mind and emotions, when the time was right liquor would reassert its dominance, take over his life again.

Well, it wouldn't dominate him again. No way. But honestly lately he drank a bit too much. There were the drinks at Hardy's Tavern with Pflam, in Spivak's office there was the whiskey. Last night with Dorothea there'd been the gin. Tight rein in the future on his intake; he'd do it, he had will power.

The clash of caste iron against a stove and Preston knew that Dorothea was up, starting breakfast. He sat up eagerly and pulled the blanket round his shoulders. He was eager to see her again. But sitting on the edge of his bed he was stopped by his thoughts. He was well past forty, women generally found him attractive, they'd always come on to him. The time with Edith, his former wife and mother of his daughter, had taught him that monogamy was not a tolerable condition for him. His encounters had always followed a similar pattern. First he'd feel growing curiosity about a particular woman. How would she react to his contact? How would she feel and sound? But when the passion was spent, sometimes even after the initial involvement, he'd feel the strong even overpowering need to be alone. Solitude would replace passion.

The attractive and energetic Leona had merely been the latest of his experiences with passion versus solitude. Leona had made the mistake of planning future meetings and his honesty had reduced her to tears. But now Dorothea had happened, she had come to him with a surprising but welcome invitation. The reactive need to be alone, the need that had left Leona in sorrow, had gone. Curiosity, the passion that had motivated his physical needs, seemed to be limited to Dorothea. He had been satisfied.

Perhaps he'd come home.

Dorothea heard his step and leaned over the warming griddle to hide her smile of anticipation. "Morning, Preston, how about some nice warm pancakes?"

The steps came closer and she felt the warmth in her face as his hands were on her waist.

"Preston," Dorothea's voice was low and uneven. "Please. Someone might come in."

He released her and stepped back as she turned to face him.

"Sorry, couldn't help myself. Needed to touch you again. Likely to be a long day, I may not be back til late."

"Where are you going?" Her hands went to her mouth. "Sorry, I don't mean to pry."

"You aren't. On some police business. I will be driving around out in the county.

"Will it be dangerous?"

He held her waist, kissing her quickly. "Just tedious," he lied.

"I'll have a plate of food for you in the oven." She kissed him back. "Be careful. Don't get stuck in any mud holes."

Preston tried to be patient as he listened to Spivak's concern for his safety.

"I've been thinking about the plan. You're putting yourself in danger and you'll be alone, vulnerable, no one to back you up if the gang gets suspicious." Milton Spivak did not look at his colleague.

Preston thought that the matter had been settled but he did not allow the impatience to show. "My big worry is getting stuck out there in the rural county. That sandy loam can get slicker than cat shit if there's rain."

"Yeah, a long walk can tire you out, but it won't get you shot. Wish you'd agree to let me get you some help. I know a guy, Clint Nivens. He's worked with this department and is a deputy with the sheriff's department. He's a solid cop."

Preston shook his head. "The car thieves won't feel threatened if I am alone and I'm used to play-acting. Done it undercover with the state police. I think it will go smoother if I do it alone. Once I've spotted them I'll be back and we can gather a posse to nab them."

Spivak shrugged and nodded. "OK, Preston, it's going to be your way." He rested his boots on his desk and teetered back in his chair. "But maybe I can still help you out a bit." He raised his hand to halt the detective's protest. "Hear me out. We agree on what might happen if it rains. And rainstorms in this season can happen pretty quick. If you get stuck out there you can't be looking for the bad guys. So come look at something."

Spivak stood up and put on his hat. "Come on with me out to the motor pool. I got a De Soto out there, about a 1937 I think. It's a heavy old thing, doesn't go very fast but it's powerful. Might get you out of a tough spot. It's green and ugly enough to suit a traveling salesman." He held the door for Preston and they walked together toward the field where the Lake Harbor Police Department parked their cars.

"Young rumrunner we stopped in the De Soto was a tough guy. Tried to shoot it out with us. Guess he figured he was bullet-proof." He laughed and slapped Preston on the back. "He wasn't. We patched up the bullet holes pretty well. "

Chapter 21

Preston's job was easy; all he had to do was drive the Ottawa county dirt roads that crossed the townships east and south of Lake Harbor, keeping his eyes open. Recent rains had left the sandy loam pocked, clearly holding the imprint of tire tracks. Just south of the city where urban buildings and angles gave way to untidy, wild growth he stopped the car, got out and walked around. The gritty sand crunched under his shoes as he knelt to look more closely at the tire marks. The depressions were smooth showing tread only at the edge of the track. Not many trucks these days ran on new tires.

He drove south slowly looking for a road heading east. Milton had given him a hand-drawn map showing a blacktopped north-south road in that direction.

Fall cold snaps had caused most of the second growth elm and aspen trees to drop their leaves. Those still attached to limbs had turned golden yellow. A breeze rustled through the brown leaves on the ground and pushed them rattling along the dirt road. Bunchgrass and dandelion weeds were slowly reestablishing their dominion over the middle of the unpaved road.

He drove past a crumbling homestead where a sumac bush formed wide crimson blanket for a crumbling wall. Uncared for apple orchards were filled with angled bare branches reaching crazily into the sky. In front of a deserted barn a mulberry tree was being slowly strangled by webworms.

Rising above other trees there were a few white pines, tall and straight as sentinels. Preston imagined the majestic forests of white pines that once covered the entire state. The shadowed quiet must have been imposing. Along the edge of the road, in the shallow ditches red poppies and golden daisies were not yet made limp and ragged by cold nights. As a typical urban dweller Preston wavered between struggling to name the flora and simply giving his senses over to the appreciation of sight and smell. Rabbits dashed for the brush after looking at the De Soto. Once a trio of whitetail does leaped across the road into the safety of the brush.

He stopped the car and went to the place where he'd seen the herd. They had appeared and disappeared so quickly and without sound that he thought there might be a hidden road. The brush was dense and he wasn't able to see anything. The only sound was the tapping of large green grasshoppers as they fled.

The sun was rising higher in the clear sky; the breeze had quieted. The air was warming. Preston took off his jacket and threw it into the car as he got in. Rubbing the sore spot on his hip, he unclipped the holster from his belt and put it and the snub-nose .38 in the glove box.

Starting up the green De Soto, he remembered Spivak's description of the car. The auto was ugly and slow. He missed the peppy Ford, but this one was powerful, less likely to get stuck.

Easing it into gear and moving ahead slowly, he realized he was starving. So intent on touching and kissing Dorothea, behaving like a school kid, he left without breakfast. Damn, she made good pancakes too. Hunger was forgotten when the car came up out of a muddy dip in the road. At the top of the climb there was a wooden house once painted white. The roof timbers had broken and the roof had fallen into the house. He spotted movement by the house and stopped opposite the wreck. A small tent was partially hidden by the brush near a low shed.

"Hello there," he called out in his most friendly salesman voice. "Anybody around? I'm lost and need some help. Hello?"

Preston had spent the quiet time while he slowly drove the roads fabricating a cover story. There was no response to his voice at first then there was a rustling sound and tree branches moved.

"Whatcher want?" A hoarse voice called out. Then a small, skinny man wearing filthy jacket over bib overalls and a ragged felt hat stepped into a clearing. A tall, skinny boy, perhaps in his teens, followed him. "I said whatcher want?"

Preston smiled and waved through the car window. "Heard you, neighbor." He lit a cigarette and puffed a cloud of smoke out the window. "OK if I get out so we can talk?"

The man nodded, took off his hat and spat. "You all got another of them smoke? Meldrick's my name." He pointed over his shoulder. "That's Jack, my boy. He don't talk much." Jack's arm remained at his side as his hand made a slight movement of greeting. Preston smiled at both of them and gave Meldrick a cigarette and lit it..

"Thanks, it's been days." He waved the smokes at Preston and took another drag. "Now what was it you was asking?"

"I'm lost. Trying to find that paved road going south. Is it this way, is it very far?"

A groan followed by pleading, "Jackie," came from the tent. The boy ran off and disappeared into the tent.

"My old lady," Meldrick gestured with his head. "She's dying, won't last much longer. Boy will see to her."

"Sorry."

Meldrick shrugged. "We're gypsies, that's what we are." He jerked his head in the direction of the moaning. "Old lady won't last much longer. Then me and the boy will move on. Nothing much to live on round here." Preston handed him another cigarette. "Thanks. You wanted to know about roads?"

Preston nodded.

"Can't tell you nothing mister. We just hike wherever we need to go. Don't know about roads and cars."

The groans were lower and spaced as Preston waved goodbye and went back to his car. He'd given Meldrick a dollar and the rest of the pack of Lucky Strikes.

As he drove away he noticed that the sky had darkened and the air was cooler. He took a westward dirt road and headed back toward town. The dark clouds moving inland reminded him of the rain and mud in France. He drove a little faster. He came over a rise and noticed movement a hundred yards in front. Near a pine twisted by a lightning strike he saw a form standing at the edge of the road. It was a solitary figure, a female of eight or nine wearing a ragged dress. She had a frayed hat on that was too big and set off by a red poppy. By her bare, filthy feet was a basket.

He slowed and came to a stop. What was a kid doing out here and rain threatening? "You got something to eat in that basket?" She didn't answer but watched him warily.

"Looks like it's going to rain, don't it?" She moved back a step but Preston saw that the basket held small red apples.

She brushed back hair that had fallen over her eyes and looked up at him past the frayed rim of her cloche. "They's a penny each. Had to walk a long way to gather them. Ain't hardly wormy at all."

They looked edible. He knelt down and selected three of them. Straightening up he polished one and bit into it. Though it was mushy and past its prime, it had some sweetness. He chewed it slowly while he dug a nickel out of his pocket and handed it to her.

Her dirty fingers closed around the coin. "Got no change. Five cents take away three equals two." She looked at him proudly. "I know my numbers and I ain't got no change."

He waited while he chewed another bite. "Don't want change. Keep it. Got a dime you can have if you help me."

She bent over in a crouch, ready to run. "What you want from me?"

"Just some information."

"Don't know much."

"Oh, I bet you're a smart girl, got sharp eyes. See much traffic on these dirt roads?"

She replied with a shrug but Preston saw that she didn't look him in the eyes. This time he would not push. Next time he'd keep an eye for her and have another try.

He held out a new dime. It lay in his palm next to a square, shiny religious medal attached to a short chain. He'd forgotten the St. Christopher medal in his pocket. The weakening sunlight glinted on the metal. "What's your name?" He asked.

"You a cop or something?"

"No need to worry about that. Just trying to be friendly. I'm

Preston."

"Can I have both of them shiny things?"

He nodded, "Sure, go ahead."

The coins disappeared into her pocket. "I'm Pen. Me and Cliffie, my brother, live over there." She pointed east. We work for Aunt and Uncle sometimes. I walk all over this country."

He would look out for her and have another talk. A look at the sky told him he'd better get back to Lake Harbor. "It's going to rain soon, Pen. You going to be all right? I can take you someplace."

"No, don't need no help at all." She backed away from the road toward the brush.

"When I see you again I'll buy some more of your apples," Preston promised as Pen went into the undergrowth.

By the time he got to town the rain had begun. He stopped at the police station to tell Spivak about his lack of success. The sergeant said they'd suspend the search for a day while the roads dried.

By the time Preston parked in front of the rooming house it was raining hard. Dorothea met him at the door.

"Ah, good, you're back." She dabbed at his wet face with a towel and gave him a quick kiss. They went into the dining room to join the others eating the hot split pea soup. Preston noticed Mordechai watching them from the shadows by the dining room door. He started to greet the rotund salesman but did not.

Chapter 22

Beneath the covers in Dorothea's double bed Preston, in shorts and undershirt, shivered and listened to the evening rain pound against the roof. He warmed up slowly, drowsing as he listened to Dorothea as she pottered about her apartment. She'd washed her face and rinsed out the coffee pot, set it on the drain board. The bottle of Gilbey's Gin clicked against the glasses as Dorothea poured them nightcaps. The firm thump of her bare feet came closer. There was the soft swish of her flannel nightgown as she sat on the mattress. Setting the drinks on the bedside table the sheets rustled as she pulled them back and slid in beside him.

"Oh, he's asleep. Poor guy worked so hard. I'll leave him alone tonight." She said in a stage whisper.

He heard her sip her drink, set it back on the table. Then there was the snip of the light switch as she turned it off. When she slid down further under the covers he caught hold of her and held her close.

"Wow, your feet are cold," he complained and laughed.

She entwined her legs in his. "Any part of me that's cold it's your fault, mister. Why don't you warm me up?" He reached across her and took a big drink of gin before he kissed her.

Preston awoke and lay in the dark listening. Warm against his side, Dorothea breathed slowly and deeply. The rain whispered against the window. He felt replete and did not want to move but remembered her concern that the roomers not know of their relationship. It was time for him to get up and go to his room. He kissed her cheek lightly and slowly drew back the covers. Setting his feet on the chill floor, Preston found his clothes and left the room. He slowly descended the stairs, his hip was sore. Recalling the activity that had caused the discomfort, he smiled. Dorothea had been a very active partner. In his own room he quickly got into the cold bed under the blankets. The prospect of spending the day with Dorothea was an attractive one. He sighed and was soon asleep.

❧ ❧ ❧

Dorothea roused when Preston threw back the blankets and slid out of bed. He probably imagined he was being quiet but he snuffled and jiggled the mattress enough to rouse even a sound sleeper. And this morning she was not sleeping very soundly.

During the first hours of the night Dorothea had slept lightly and roused often as her mind reran images of her and Preston together. The physical contact was very nice. Preston, with his jokes and teasing seemed to her to be like a little boy in a man's body. He laughed and was a delight.

He tiptoed across the floor and when the door clicked shut she rolled over and looked at the clock. There was time for some sleep before she had to start breakfast. She hoped Preston would be able to join everyone for the meal and not have to run off on police work.

❧ ❧ ❧

Preston was jolted awake by the call from the kitchen that breakfast was ready. He was irritated with himself because he'd planned to go down to the kitchen with Dorothea and help. He'd overslept, but as he rushed to dress he resolved to help her clean up after the meal.

Wearing wrinkled trousers and an old shirt, he hurried as fast as his hip would allow him down the stairs and quickly sat at the table with the others. Acutely aware that his hair stood up and he'd not shaved, Dorothea's smile and the greetings from the other guests made him relax.

The warm oatmeal with butter and cinnamon was a treat. His mother had often made cooked cereal for breakfast when the weather got cold. He had a big bowl and two slices of toast. As he finished his coffee the roomers rose, said goodbye and went to get their coats from the hall closet.

"Be sure and dress warmly, take an umbrella. It's still drizzling," He heard Dorothea advise them.

"I guess there's just the two of us," he commented as he helped her gather up dirty dishes.

She chuckled as she worked at the sink. "Abandoned. Orphans is what we is." Rumpled Preston felt a bit like a little boy.

They easily slipped into the routine of washing the dishes.

Dorothea scrubbed the dishes in the soap and water then rinsed them in the second sink. Preston dried the dishes and stacked them on the table.

"I'm not going out today. Yesterday Sergeant Spivak advised me not to drive if it rained much. He's afraid I'll get stuck and have to walk back to town."

Dorothea nodded in agreement. "Milton Spivak's a careful fellow. After a hard rain those roads can become mud wallows."

"So you'll have to put up with me."

"That'll be a chore, but I think I can handle it." Finished, she dried her hands and turned to face him. A sly smile lit up her face. "How much do you know about housework?"

"Oh, oh, I think I'm about to learn a lot more."

"Well, Preston, you can't be a policeman today so you'll learn how to be a maid." She laughed a bit at his scowl. "My clients have to fend for themselves for lunch. I use the time to clean up this place."

"I'll help," Preston said.

She took him by the arm and walked around showing him the area rugs that needed shaking. "Take them out to the back yard and snap them good." When he was finished he looked at the pile and was stumped about where to put them.

"You sure you don't mind housework?" Dorothea asked him again. She patted his arm. "Don't worry about it. Pick them up and I'll show you where they go." When the rugs were back in place, she asked him again, "you don't mind the work?"

"Nope, strangely enough I kind of like the exercise. I was ready for some activity. Sitting in the car all day makes me stiff. I feel like an old man."

"Well Methuselah, put down that rag and come on into the kitchen and sit down. I've made some sandwiches, you've earned a break."

She'd made fried egg sandwiches. With hot leftover coffee the meal was comforting on a chilly day.

As they ate they commented on the dark, low clouds over the lake. Dorothea observed, "I bet we get some more rain today. Don't expect it will be too much. The main part of the storm has passed over."

"That's bad news. I had hoped we might take a walk by the lake."

"Sounds nice but I'm afraid it wouldn't be very comfortable," she replied as gusts buffeted the kitchen window.

After they had finished the sandwiches they sat at the table in the kitchen. Preston looked at the window where an occasional raindrop splashed. She thought a moment. "I don't want to pry but why do you need to drive around out there? Looking for something?"

"I'm helping Spivak investigate car thefts. Big expensive cars are being stolen. They simply disappear. Usually stolen cars turn up after a few days. Young fellows out for a thrill take them and leave them when they're through playing. These cars haven't showed up again."

"What could happen to them?" Dorothea asked.

"Don't know for sure but it could be that a gang of hoodlums is taking them to sell to bank robbers."

"But what's that got to do with driving around out in the county?"

"Pflam and I met up with a snitch in a low-life tavern, He told us he'd heard of a gang working near here in the county. So we're looking for them. Their hideout may be out in the county."

"Is there anybody out there?"

"Some down-and-out folks. There was a young girl alone, but she said her brother was with her."

"All by herself?" She looked at the rain spotted window and shivered. "Hope she and her brother have a warm place tonight." She thought for a minute. "Noah has taken you to some of his favorite taverns?"

"Just one. Hardy's was the name. It's a real dive but it's where we met the snitch."

"Hardy's Tavern? Pflam took you there?"

"Yeah, you know it?"

"Sure, I've been there."

Preston turned away and looked out the window. She got up. "More coffee, dear?" The face he turned toward her was distorted by anger.

"Why, Preston, whatever is the matter?"

"You've been to Hardy's?"

"Yes."

"It is a hangout for whores and criminals. I have no idea why somebody I thought was a lady would spend time among such people. I don't want you ever going there again." His words were uttered with a strangled kind of intensity that threatened to erupt like a volcano,

Dorothea felt the heat rise to her head while her ears

hummed. "Listen to me, Mister Duhamel, I have been to Hardy's. I went alone and returned the same way. I talked to the whores and the criminals as well as the workmen and their wives. Went there to try to find people who might need a room and could pay the pittance I charge. Went there to find roomers so as to keep my business going."

His voice was low when he answered. "Yes, of course, I should have known. I apologize. I was not thinking."

Dorothea's words rose in anger. "Yes, you should have thought. This lady is a businesswoman who runs her own place and is her own boss. You are welcome to my bed but only on the basis of equality. I am not yours to push around. No boss, no one in charge, we are equal. And if you can't handle that then pack up your bags and be gone. The bit you owe is my gift to you."

He bowed his head and stared at his hands resting on the table.

"Well, what is it? Accept my terms or go, Preston." She turned in her chair to the window and stared at the gray expanse of the lake

He rose and went to the stove. Picking up the coffee pot he returned to the table. "Can I pour you some fresh?"

Chapter 23

Preston poured more coffee for them both. After placing the pot on the stove he returned to his seat opposite Dorothea. Through the window he saw that the day remained overcast and gray. Rain tapped at the window and he heard the waves breaking against the beach.

"You were right. This is no day for walking."

Dorothea gave him a preoccupied look and nod.

After a long silence Dorothea rose and checked the soup pot on the stove. Almost as an afterthought she looked at her lover.

"Shall we go on with the housework or are you tired?" she asked.

"Not tired at all," he replied. "I'm ready for more." He patted his game hip. "I'll last a little longer if there aren't a lot of stairs to climb." There was a nervous edge to his laugh.

"Oh, dear," Dorothea looked at the broom standing in the corner.

"Just the tool I'm really good with." He got up and took hold of the broom. "I'll sweep the kitchen, shall I?"

"And the porch if you will, Preston." She made a mental

note to sweep the back stairs herself another time. Then she added tentatively, "dear."

Grateful to be past the silences and to be busy at a task that would please Dorothea, Preston set to work.

He'd been with other women who resented being ordered about. Some had protected their integrity as sharply as had Dorothea. But he couldn't remember feeling endangered by them. When an affair ended he just moved on. Then there'd been others who had tried to control him with their bodies and tears.

"Preston, please," he remembered Leona pleading as she had held his jacket lapels at the door when he was leaving. "I must see you again. You feel the same way; what we shared was nice, right?"

Leona, inspector Finley's secretary, did look inviting with her dark hair mussed and her robe not quite closed. But he was on assignment.

"Leona, honey, we had a great time but I don't know where I'll be stationed. But I tell you what, when my boss lets me get settled maybe I'll write."

She cuddled against him. The warmth of the bed they'd shared still clung to her body. "Write me and I'll come see you," she murmured.

"I may be moving around so you won't hear from me for awhile." Preston knew he would not see her again. It wouldn't be long and a good-looking woman like her would find a new love.

The conflict with Dorothea just a few minutes ago was a new experience for him and it opened a surprising set of emotions. He experienced fear when she uttered her ultimatum; he did not want to go. Somewhere in his heart he knew that leaving would end something important. His silent capitulation had been more decisive than a spoken apology and had been as natural as it was surprising.

As he swept the floor he peeked at Dorothea as she heated the evening meal: vegetable soup. Humming she sliced an onion into the broth and added some meat stock saved from a previous meal. Everything she did was planned, decisive; that was how she was. Finishing his work with the broom, Preston cleaned up after her, sliced bread, and made coffee. Then he made sure the dining room was ready, places set.

"It's after five," she said and shivered. "Rain has stopped. Hope the guests haven't gotten wet through." As if in response to Dorothea's concern, the front door opened and Beryl and Minnie came in chatting. They stopped to watch Preston and Dorothea a moment then climbed the stairs giggling. The front door opened and Mordechai returned. He peered at them, nodded and went up to his room. A quiet Nils followed. The twin blows of losing his friend, Clement, and his brother's arrest in Denmark had depressed him.

When she called up the stairway to the roomers, their response was lethargic. Perhaps because of the chill, blustery weather all of them, Mordechai McNeil, Nils Nilson, Beryl Richards and Minnie Quinton, seemed tired, a bit bedraggled. Greeting Dorothea and Preston they sat at their places and ate. There was little conversation, silence broken only by the soft slurping of the hot soup.

Preston sat down to his meal and was surprised by his weariness; the yawns would not stop coming. After one that strained his jaw and left his eyes tearing he saw Dorothea looking at him. He smiled and shrugged. She smiled back and it seemed to him that she too was tired.

The emotions that had been generated by the argument earlier seemed to have emotionally drained her. Dorothea felt that it had been best to draw the lines now before the affair progressed. He had to be clear about who she was and what she wanted in her life. She'd worked too hard, invested too much energy in her business to let anyone take it away from her. To her it was far more than fixing hot meals and keeping a clean rooming house. She'd learned from Grannie Quinn that caring for her people had no limits.

Preston was looking at her. Dorothea nodded in response. His dark eyes seemed sunken, weary; she smiled. Perhaps she'd been too hard on him. He had such a nice smile. Looking away she hoped they could work it out.

Meal finished, Preston carried the dishes to the kitchen while Dorothea talked with Beryl and Minnie. The old ladies had some questions for her about California and the West. Mordechai and Nils climbed the stairs to their rooms.

Dorothea went into the kitchen to help him with the dishes. Beryl and Minnie went into the front room, and sat on the couch, discussing the details of the latest adventures of the Lone Ranger. They were devout fans of the radio program and regularly listened to it in the social room.

Preston and Dorothea had just finished tidying up the kitchen when the doorbell rang. She looked through the peephole then opened it.

"Sorry if it's too late." Opal Meacham spoke, smiling down at Dorothea's shoes.

"It's not that late, come on in, Opal." Dorothea stood back

from the door and invited her next-door neighbor in.

Opal nodded and reached behind her to tug at a slender form. She urged a youngster of fourteen into the foyer. "Sorry, I got Emma, my sister's child, with me. She's plain shy and that's the truth."

Dorothea surveyed the girl. Emma bobbed a quick curtsey when her aunt pushed her. She hugged a cheap suitcase as if she were trying to disappear behind it. She wore a shapeless cotton dress faded to an indeterminate color that barely reached her knees. A threadbare coat closed with mismatched buttons protected her from the evening cold.

Opal looked at Emma and shook her head in frustration. She turned to Dorothea and explained. "We're so late cause I had to work. Emma waited all day in the bus station until I could get her. Wanted to bring her over, maybe you could tell her about her duties. I can't come with her in the morning, I got to go to work early."

"I'm glad you brought her. Let's go to the kitchen where we can be more comfortable." She took Emma's suitcase and set it on the floor. Holding the girl's hand she led them toward the kitchen. "Preston," she called out, "there's some coffee left isn't here?"

"Yep, I'll heat it up," he replied.

"It's been a long day for both of you. Have a cup and then we'll talk about work. How about something to eat? I got some soup."

"Gee, Dorothea, we don't want to be no bother." The looks both guests gave the food told Dorothea they were hungry. Preston stood at the door. Dorothea took his hand, pressed it indicating by gesture that she wanted to talk to the visitors alone. He nodded and went up the stairs to his room.

When the three women were seated at the small table in the kitchen Dorothea poured coffee, sliced bread and set out some margarine. Then she got out bowls and spooned soup into them. Emma could scarcely control her eagerness as she buttered a slice, devoured it as she eagerly emptied the bowl. She then took big drink of the strong coffee and sighed.

"Oh, thanks, Miss Dolan, I was near starved for sure." She whispered.

"Emma, dear," Opal disciplined her niece, "hush and listen to what Miss Dolan tells you."

Dorothea saw that the girl could not keep her eyes from the remaining bread. She pushed the plate closer to her.

While Emma munched on a slice of bread Dorothea explained that she wanted her to help with the serving of meals and the house cleaning. As she talked the girl chewed and nodded to indicate she'd heard.

When Emma looked straight at her, Dorothea almost forgot what she was explaining. The girl had the features of an angel. Blue eyes, perfect complexion and naturally red lips were enough to demand a second look from anyone. Were her hair freed from the yarn used to tie it back surely it would frame her heart-shaped face with a reddish halo. When Emma sat up straight in the chair to stretch her back it was clear that she was a well-developed young woman.

Beryl came to the doorway and got Dorothea's attention. "Lone Ranger and Tonto are safe. We're going up now, tired. Evening news is nothing but war and destruction. That Hitler fellow is sure scary. Those Nazis have all of Europe seems like."

Dorothea introduced the visitors, "Beryl you remember Opal, our neighbor. Her niece Emma is going to help me out."

Beryl took Emma's hand, "You'll be working for a mighty fine lady, miss. Night all." Together Beryl and Minnie went into the shadows to the back staircase and up to their rooms.

Emma in quick, surreptitious movements ate two more slices of bread. When she was told that she would be expected to help with breakfast Emma smiled and became animated.

"I got up real early in Detroit, Miss. Worked in a shirt factory. Machines went on at five sharp so I know how to wake myself up. I always woke up the family. Mom relied on me." She bowed her head again.

Opal was quick to support Emma. "She's a good girl, Dorothea. Very dependable. Had a good job but – well – it's best for her to stay with me for a while."

Emma raised her head and Dorothea saw that her eyes were moist. "If I'm over here then maybe they won't argue so much."

"That's enough, Emma. No need to wash family linen in public." Opal squeezed Emma's hand and gave Dorothea a conspiratorial look. "I've got a room where she can sleep. That box room. We'll clean it out good. Thanks for giving the girl work. You can rely on her." As they rose from the table Opal took Dorothea's hand and shook it. Emma curtseyed and thanked Dorothea. Then they were gone.

In his room asleep, Preston felt her kiss as if he were dreaming. He rolled over and snuggled under the covers as Dorothea left and went to her own bed.

Chapter 24

The sky was still dark when Dorothea came down to fix break-fast. Yawning she put the coffee on as she heard a noise coming from the front step. The peephole revealed Emma dancing about. The poor girl had on her worn coat with the mismatched buttons. Dorothea tugged open the door.

"Emma, get in here. You're going to freeze solid. Why didn't you ring the bell?" Her words as she unlocked the door came out a bit harsher than she meant them to. Dorothea felt a bit guilty leaving the girl out in the cold.

"It's all right, didn't want to disturb anybody. Me and Aunt Opal wanted to make sure I got here early to help." Emma's lips were blue and her teeth chattered as she spoke.

Dorothea led Emma back to the kitchen. The room still held some warmth from the night before. The coffee was boiling and now there was the batter to prepare. The girl followed Dorothea around the kitchen learning about the breakfast routine. After being shown where the dishes and the utensils were Emma rushed to set the table. She offered to stir the batter but Dorothea preferred to do that herself.

"You get yourself a cup, pour yourself some coffee and sit down while I stir. Soon there'll be more than enough work."

Dorothea smiled at the eager youngster.

Emma watched her stir with the big wooden spoon while she sipped hot coffee. "Mmm, good," she whispered.

"Did you sleep well?" Dorothea asked.

"I slept sound, sure enough. Course Aunt Opal don't have a proper bed yet for me. There's just a pallet of blankets but I got my own room. In Detroit I never had a room of my own. Had to share with Alvy and Benny, my brothers."

Dorothea had visited Opal Meacham's house and remembered that the storage or box room where Emma slept last night was not much bigger than a closet but the youngster seemed thrilled with the accommodations.

When the guests started moving around upstairs Dorothea poured dollops of batter onto the griddle. Emma rushed about saving Dorothea steps. As the roomers came into the dinning room she helped them get seated and was rewarded with a chorus of pleased reactions.

"Just set the butter over here young lady. I like my coffee hot and plenty of butter on my cakes." Nils was particularly taken with Emma. "Thank you," his deep voice grumbled, "Come over here," he ordered as he held out his hand. "Now you just take this."

"Miss Dolan," the girl rushed into the kitchen where Dorothea was working at the griddle. "Mister – ah – Nils, he give me a nickel." She held the coin out in her palm.

"Nils is a generous fellow," Dorothea responded as she turned the pancakes.

"Ought I to keep it?"

"Emma, you earned it, so put it in your pocket. I'll bet Nils and the others would like some more cakes." She held out a platter full. Emma grabbed it and hurried into the dining room.

"Well, hello sleepyhead," Dorothea greeted Preston as he stumbled into the room. She looked at him closely. "Well, that's a little better. Your hair is combed and you've shaved."

"Yeah, but I overslept again." He came close to Dorothea and touched her shoulder. "This morning I found lipstick on my cheek. You wouldn't know who left it there, would you?"

"Why Mister Duhamel, whatever are you talking about." She affected a Scarlett O'Hara accent. In her own voice she ordered, "you'd better get in there before they eat it all."

As he seated himself at the table Dorothea heard the gruff compliments Nils offered to Emma. Minnie raised her voice slightly as she held the girl's arm after Emma had sung a short ditty for her. "Why child you have a beautiful voice. This evening we'll have a sing-along and I want to hear you nice and loud." Beryl giggled behind her hand. Emma blushed and curtseyed. Mordechai watched as he drank his coffee.

Preston had finished his first pancake when the phone rang.

Sergeant Milton Spivak's office in the Lake Harbor city police station was cold. "I told the chief," he said slouching in his chair, "that we ought to go into the butcher business. Hang sides of beef in here and they'd never spoil. I got some good news. Maybe help us forget the chill."

When the detective was seated Spivak asked if he was

hungry. He gestured toward a box of doughnuts on his desk.

"No, thanks, Milton, I had breakfast before I came over. Dorothea was frying flapjacks."

Spivak smacked his lips. "That lady knows how to cook, right? Got to sneak over there for breakfast one day soon." He lit a cigarette and tossed the pack to Preston. "Now my Sadie – a fine woman – but she's missing some chapters in her cookbook."

As Preston lit his cigarette the cop sat up. "I thought you'd want to be here."

Preston leaned forward and wished his friend would get on with it.

"Noah Pflam dragged that sorry excuse for a man – Flip Delanty – in here this morning. Seems he saved Flip from some guys intent on smashing his skull." The sergeant stopped to sip his coffee. "The hoodlums had a chance to rearrange Flip's face. Two of them gave him quite a beating before Noah saved his bacon. Pflam shot one but they got away. Seems that the disagreement involved stolen cars so thought you'd like to be in on the interrogation."

"You read my mind, Sergeant."

"Pflam saved his life so maybe Flip would like to share some information. Could be a break for us."

Preston nodded and rose to follow the sergeant down a dim hallway.

Milton opened the door to a long room bisected by a scarred table and some chairs. At the far end of the table a man raised his head when they entered. His head was wrapped in white bandages. A dark bruise closed his right eye. With a handkerchief he wiped his left eye and blinked at them.

Spivak spoke, "The police surgeon got you fixed up and we're going to talk."

"We need a crowd, do we?" Flip growled the question to Pflam who sat next to him and was smiling at Preston.

Pflam stood and smartly saluted to his superiors. "Now Flip, old boy, you don't need to be disrespectful. These men are here to help you." Spivak motioned for him to sit down.

Pflam lit a cigarette and gave it to Delanty then he looked at the two men who were just sitting down. "My friend Flip here forgets that two rascals were ready to make like 'Hammering Hank' Greenberg of our beloved Tigers. The one I winged had a ball bat and was just winding up going to knock his bean out of the park. Good thing I happened by, weren't it?" Delanty grunted in response.

"The one you shot got away did he?" Spivak questioned.

The officer ducked his head. "Ashamed to admit, the two scoundrels made off. They were driving a black Ford club coupe. Couldn't make out the license plate. It was covered with mud. The whole vehicle was covered with mud."

Preston figured that were the fight connected to the auto thieving then the muddy auto probably meant they been right in supposing that the crooks were hiding among the empty farms. He might have driven past their hideout already.

"Pay attention, Flip, I got some questions for you. And I want straight answers," Spivak barked out the orders as if he were on the parade ground.

The battered man cursed. "My head hurts."

"Then answer the questions so you can go lay down with some nice coffee, and have a pill for the pain, right Pflam?" The officer nodded quickly.

"Why'd these guys beat you?"

"They were trying to take my money." Delanty's voice was sarcastic.

Spivak never took his eyes off Delanty. "Pflam, how much did this liar have on him?"

"Not enough to buy a dollar supper, Sergeant."

Spivak gazed at the beaten man for a long moment. "Why don't you be nice to yourself, Flip? Stop protecting the scum trying to kill you."

"OK, I might have heard something. But if I tell you then they'll know I squealed and they'll come back to finish the job."

"Not if they're in the slammer. Besides I'll assign Pflam here to protect you til we get those fellows locked up. You can bunk in one of our deluxe cells. Three hot squares a day until your friends are in the penitentiary. I promise."

Flip's single eye was bloodshot. He wiped it again and sighed. "I heard something and they know it. They was in a game of craps in the alley there. With two other guys but they run off when the tough guys jumped on me."

Flip took a drag. "They all was rolling dice and I saw them. I just kind of eased up close in the shadows and listened."

"Go ahead. What did you hear?"

"Those two, Jo-Jo and Tommy is what they called themselves, they was bragging about lucking into a real good racket. They heisted cars and then sold them to bank robbers in Chicago and about."

"So they beat you for that?"

"Well, I heard that they worked for some tough old bird who used to crack safes. Mean old guy by the name of Delbert. Got a scar on his face and lost a little finger. It got crushed when he was ripping the back off of one of those old safes."

He rested his bandaged head on his hand as if it had grown heavy. "Tommy saw me and yelled. "'Christ, he's a snitch. Delbert will kill us.' And then they came after me."

Preston looked at Milton and they smiled at each other.

Chapter 25

Outside of Lake Harbor driving east away from Lake Michigan Preston reminded himself to ease up on the gas. The day was warmer and the winds were drying out the puddles but he still should be careful. His mind kept running over the new information about the car thieves and the excitement seemed to travel down his right leg making his foot press harder against the accelerator. The excitement was making him forgetful too. This morning Dorothea had had to run to bring his forgotten lunch and thermos out to the car before he pulled away. She'd included a sack of bread and and a few potatoes for the young girl, Pen, Preston had befriended.

Delanty had described the gang leader, providing details that would make the head thief easier to spot. If Preston put in the hours and drove enough roads he'd spot an older guy, probably with broad shoulders, named Delbert who was missing a little finger and had a scar on his face. Probably Delbert would be with two hooligans named Tommy and Jo-Jo.

"Pay attention," he reminded himself aloud.

Fortunately for him the sandy clay roads were not too treacherous despite the recent rain. As he glanced in the rear view mirror he saw the reason for the dryness; the road sloped up gradually as he left the lake. The incline was not great, though enough to drain the road surface.

As he drove on he passed some north-south roads and saw that they were muddy and in low places deep sloughs had formed. Even in the sloppiest looking spots he figured that if he hugged the east side of the road he could get through.

The morning clouds broke up and gradually blew away. The sun was bright though the air was cold. His snub-nose .38 in a clip-on belt holster chafed his hip so he slid the gun and holster off his belt and left it on the passenger seat beneath his jacket.

In the distance to his left he recognized the damaged bare-topped pine tree where he had talked with Pen. He wondered what the youngster was doing; did she have more apples? Had the St. Christopher medal brought Pen any luck? Today on the way back he'd go past that tree and maybe he'd see her again. Pen was about ten, the same age as Solange, his daughter. Was Solange so tall? He'd not seen her since she was five.

He passed the ruined house where he'd talked with the fellow whose wife was sick. What was his name, Melton? No, Meldrick. And he'd had a boy by the name of Jackie who didn't talk.

The tent that was Meldrick's wife's makeshift hospital room was gone. Preston wondered if the poor woman was buried nearby.

Recent rain and warmer than usual weather had reinvigorated the flora. Red poppies were everywhere as were tall sunflowers and white daisies. Bird-pecked fruit weighed down apple tree branches no long tended. Wildlife benefited from the late growth. He saw plump shy whitetail does with their fawns. Everywhere rabbits bounded away as his car approached.

After a long drive east Preston came upon a two lane paved highway. He checked the map that Milton Spivak had given him. It wasn't very clear and most of the roads weren't identified by sign or on the map but he guessed that the pavement ran south southeast toward Illinois.

If the car thieves had a place nearby to stash the stolen vehicles, they could drive the vehicles to this paved road. Customers might come for their purchases or the thieves could deliver.

He turned left on the road and drove northwest. After driving for a short time he spotted nothing that seemed suspicious: there was no sign of traffic, no mud tracks entering the pavement from side roads. Easing the Ford onto the edge of the road he stopped and got out. Beneath a small grove of white pines he walked about smoking a cigarette. His stomach reminded him of the lunch bag on the rear seat. Preston ground out the butt with his heel. The tense excitement of the morning had dissipated during the dull hours of driving; now he was sleepy. He thought he might stretch out on the car seat and take a nap.

More clouds were moving in from the west, low and dark, threatening rain. If it started coming down he'd have an excuse to hurry back to the rooming house. Hearing a sharp, repitive noise Preston crouched down behind ditch-side weeds. The sound was a dog's barking, scared or perhaps warning. Still crouching Preston speculated that the animal could be a stray. He waited and heard an irate voice shouting, cursing. The barking stopped, followed by a yip of pain and then silence.

Preston crept back to the car and got his revolver. Without taking his gaze from the road he slipped the holster onto his belt. Ahead the road made a slight turn to the east. Foliage might hide him and the car if whoever had done the yelling came onto the road beyond the turn. He moved closer to the cover of the weeds.

Now there was an unfamiliar jangling. After a tense moment he saw two stout plow horses harnessed together, carrying a singletree, enter the highway in their strong, deliberate manner. A short, limping figure wearing ragged work clothes and a slouch hat followed the horses. A tall broad shouldered man also in work clothes and cap walked beside the limping man. A cowed brown dog followed the men.

Preston saw that the limping one was a boy of maybe fifteen. The boy yelled "Gee" to the horses and they turned to the right away from Preston. The taller fellow was carrying a rifle. Preston waited, scarcely breathing, until the pair was out of sight.

In the Ford Preston sat down but did not close the door.

He hadn't gotten a good look at the big fellow but from the way he carried himself and the broadness of his back Preston guessed he was in pretty good shape. Safecrackers, especially the ones employed to tear off the riveted backs of safes with crowbars, were often big, strong fellows. He'd have to get closer to that guy and see his hands.

They weren't suspects necessarily. But he'd have to check them out. Why had the one been armed? Hunting something for supper? Or was he on the lookout?

What about the horses? They were still widely used in farming and to free stuck autos. The animals did not make those fellows criminals but they did give him an idea of how he could check them out.

❧   ❧   ❧

"Come on, get in." On his way back to town Preston had spotted Pen sitting alongside the road. He stopped the Ford, pushed open the passenger door and invited her in.

A fresh poppy decorated her shapeless hat that shadowed her face. She wore the same clothes she'd had on when they met. Over her shoulders she'd knotted a large ragged piece of terry cloth to provide some warmth. She didn't move toward the car.

"Come on, Pen, I won't hurt you. I've got some sandwiches."

The offer of food made Pen hop up and get into the car. She closed the door but sat as far from Preston as she could on the bench seat. Pen winced and drew back when he reached back to get the bag and thermos. Preston saw that what he thought was a shadow on the side of her face was a dark bruise.

"You fell." She didn't answer but stayed close to the door hiding her cheek. "Ah, we're in luck. Pen, there's three sandwiches. Let's see what we have, shall we?" On thick slices of homemade bread, carefully wrapped in waxed paper, Dorothea had made two sliced beef sandwiches. On the third sandwich she had spread strawberry preserves. As he examined the meal he saw out of the corner of his eye the girl licking her lips and swallowing.

"Here you take this one." He handed her a beef sandwich. Pen took it, tore it in two and rewrapped half in the wax paper.

"For my brother. Sometimes Uncle Del doesn't give him much for supper. And Teddy's a growing boy," she primly finished her explanation. As she chewed she looked up at Preston, "My brother never grew up in his head. I got to take care of him."

Preston's heart gave a jump hearing Pen use the name Del. Was she connected with the gang of thieves?

Pen finished her half of the meal and the bit Preston gave

her from his. Preston drank black coffee from the thermos cup, telling Pen that he was full.

After dividing the bread and preserves, wrapping half for her brother, she devoured the rest. Preston shared his cup of coffee with her.

"Ah," the sound conveyed her satisfaction. She handed him the empty cup and relaxed against the seat. "Thank you, Preston," she whispered.

"You're welcome." He rejected the urge to give the little girl a hug and patted her hand when he took back the thermos cup. They both took care of the people fate had put in their control.

Preston lit a cigarette and waited.

"Preston, why're you driving around out here? There ain't nothing. And you brought a meal."

"There's some bread and potatoes in a sack for you too." She nodded and waited for his answer. "I'm a salesman. Sell tires and come out here to test drive new ones and I like to get away from town."

Pen nodded and thought for a while. "You'll be moving on soon then."

"Yeah, probably. Got to go where there's business." The lies did not come easy. "You going to hang around here?"

She looked out the door window and rubbed a silvery medallion pinned to her shirt. "Yeah, I suppose. Me and Teddie stay in a shed. Uncle Del and Aunt Pru let us sleep there. Teddie's good with the horses and such. When it gets real cold maybe we'll find somewhere else."

Preston took a deep breath so his voice wouldn't quaver.

"Do you help out your Aunt and Uncle?"

"Naw, they got no use for me. I just stay out of the way. There's two guys, friends of Uncle, I don 't trust them at all."

Still struggling to control his voice, Preston said, "Pen, tell me exactly where your shed is."

Chapter 26

"We got them. I know where they are." The sergeant looked up the surprise on his face turning to a smile as Preston threw open his office door.

"Sit down." Spivak brushed aside the papers he'd been working on and sat back. "Now tell me all about it."

"There's a dirt road. It's not easy to spot, almost overgrown. But push aside some branches and there's a dirt road leading to a paved one that leads south-southeast." Preston did not mention Pen or her brother. He'd make sure that they were not considered part of the gang when the arrests were made. They were just kids, Del and the rest of the gang kept them around as part of their cover. When they had the gang in the slammer Preston promised himself he'd find out who'd hit Pen.

"Toward Chicago, those guys don't miss much do they?" Spivak mused. "They've got an easy way to move the stolen cars."

"I haven't been there yet but I know where Del and his two henchmen are hanging out. Got a good description and know the layout," Preston added, hoping Spivak would not demand to know the source of the knowledge.

Spivak leaned over his desk and moved the papers about until he found the one he was looking for. "Ah, thought there was something here for us." He held up a typescript. "Our crooks may be branching out. This is report from the Muskegon police: almost new Packard stolen last week. A fancy touring sedan, Packard Super 8-180 holds seven. Black. Asks us to be on the lookout."

"Well maybe we can return that one to its owner."

"Hope so," Spivak lit up one of the little cigars he favored. "How do you think we should handle this?"

"With this threat of rain I don't think they'll be moving any autos. While you organize a posse at this end I'd like to go back and take a good look at the farmhouse, reconnoiter, see what we can expect. Maybe we can pull this off without a shootout."

Spivak was hesitant, "OK, Preston." He smiled as he blew out a cloud of smoke. "It'll break some of those deputies' hearts if there's no shoot out. But we can live with that disappointment. Don't take too long. We better wrap that gang up in a few days."

❧ ❧ ❧

"Mister – ah – Preston," Emma swallowed a mouthful of food, struggled with his last name and settled for the first. "I was just having my supper. Miss Dolan said I could eat in the kitchen." She looked more wonderingly at his muddy, disheveled appearance. She looked down at the well-gnawed pork chop bone in her right hand. "She said I could have this here piece of meat."

"Relax, Emma, you are doing just fine. I thought I'd sneak in and change clothes, not disturb the others." Preston tried to soothe the small, gentle creature looking at him as if she expected to be led away in handcuffs.

"Preston, you're wet." Dorothea came through the door.

He looked down at his dripping jacket. "Oh, no, how'd that happen?" They laughed while Emma looked on confused and still chewing.

After a quick hug when Emma wasn't looking, Preston hastened up the stairs to his room and changed into dry clothes. The journey back down to the dining room was slower. His enthusiasm had brought on the ache in his hip.

Emma had finished her meal and was washing the dishes when Preston entered the kitchen again. Dorothea hurried into the room and took Preston's hand.

"Come in to the dining room. We're having a musical evening," she explained.

She hurried back into the kitchen as he sat at the table. "I'll bring you your supper."

Minnie Quinton was seated at the piano in charge of the entertainment. She turned and shouted over her shoulder. "Child, Emma, come on in here. Sing us a song." In a stage whisper to Beryl she said, "That girl has a lovely voice. Remember? We heard her this morning?" Her friend nodded and giggled.

Emma was blushing as she came into the dining room drying her hands on a dishtowel. Behind her Dorothea gave her a little push and took the cloth. Beryl rose and scurried to the girl's side urging her to stand beside the piano.

Minnie gave a small wave and spoke. "Emma, tell me what you'd like to sing."

Wringing her hands, Emma looked at the floor and said nothing.

"Go ahead, child, I know just about any song ever sung." From her seat on the sofa Beryl leaned forward and patted Emma.

Emma's lips moved. From the dinner table Preston saw the short, rotund form of Mordechai McNeil rise and move into the front room.

"Just a little louder, Emma. I didn't hear you, honey. Let everyone enjoy your lovely voice." Minnie urged and the girl's lips moved again.

"That's a good one. I'll warm up and you start wherever you want." Minnie began to play a lilting melody. Emma started, stumbled and stopped. In a moment Minnie started the tune again and Emma sang.

> You are my sunshine
>
> My only sunshine
>
> You make me happy
>
> When skies are grey.
>
> You'll never know, dear,
>
> How much I love you.
>
> Please don't take my sunshine away

She sang the first three stanzas in a clear and true soprano. A moment of silence followed her recital and then everyone applauded. She curtseyed, and, after receiving compliments hurried back to the kitchen.

Preston felt Dorothea's touch as she leaned over him and placed a plate of carrots, potatoes and a small chop in front of him.

He was suddenly aware that he was famished and ate his supper rapidly. As he sipped his hot coffee he listened to the pleasant low chatter going on in the two rooms.

By the piano Dorothea was chatting with Minnie and Beryl. Nils slept in his usual seat on the sofa. Mordechai sat alone in a chair watching the proceedings. He got up deliberately and approached Preston.

"Sir," Preston looked up into a smiling, cherubic face, "At your service, sir. We have not had a chance to chat and I would like to rectify that error." Preston struggled to stand.

"Please," Mordechai gestured to the unoccupied chair next to Preston. "I'll join you if I may."

Preston shook the proffered hand. McNeil's grip was soft and moist. Mordechai sat down. Preston observed him and thought he looked like an aged, round, soft child. Mordechai was trying to be friendly but Preston couldn't overcome a sense of dislike for the man.

"Finish your coffee, Preston. May I call you Preston?" Mordechai waited for his nod and chattered on. "The lady makes a fine supper. The coffee is particularly pleasing. I must say that I mightily enjoyed my first meals here and look forward to many more."

"Yes, she is. Miss Dolan is a fine cook for sure." He looked toward the kitchen hoping to see Dorothea returning from the kitchen and rescuing him.

Mordechai pushed the utensils aside and rested his elbows on the table. "Preston, I am a traveling salesman. I sell fine glass-ware, stemware, silverware anything for the table of the discerning home or hotel." He smiled up at his companion and adjusted his cuffs. "Alas, as you can see I am no longer young so must slow down. Not travel so much and enjoy the autumn of my stay on earth."

He offered Preston a Lucky Strike cigarette, took one himself and lit both. "I was traveling through Lake Harbor meeting with some potential customers and learned that Miss Dolan had a room available. I shall continue selling locally while keeping my eyes open for alternative means of support. I'd appreciate your consideration were you to hear of any jobs opening up locally."

"I'll keep that in mind, Mordechai, but there's not many jobs around."

"I appreciate that but I'll take my chances and hope the good Lord favors me. In my time I've done just about every kind of work there is." He chuckled and his jowls shook. "May I inquire as to your line of work, Preston?"

He took a final sip of coffee. "Mordechai, I'm in law enforcement, with the state police on temporary assignment with the local authorities."

"Oh, my word, how exciting. I must be careful and mindful of all laws. I would not like you cuffing me." He wheezed in laughter as Preston looked around for Dorothea. He stopped his laughter abruptly and tugged at the policeman's sleeve. "We must talk again, sir."

When she came back to the table Mordechai rose, bowed and excused himself to join Beryl and Minnie at the piano. After a short patriotic speech in support of the brave British Tommies, Mordechai's strong tenor voice led the boarders in a rousing song.

Over there, over there

Send the word, send the word over there,

That the Yanks are coming,

The Yanks are coming over there.

"He's got a nice voice, doesn't he?" Dorothea said as she sat beside him.

Preston nodded and yawned. "It's been a busy day."

She gave him a coy look and said, "Emma's gone and the kitchen is cleaned up. I was hoping to find someone to come up and have a nightcap with me."

Chapter 27

Dorothea opened the door of her electric refrigerator. She'd purchased the used Crosly Shelvador at a sheriff's auction of the household chattels of a bank-foreclosed farmhouse. The shining white appliance was lovely as well as practical. She could buy extra food at sales and be sure the supplies wouldn't spoil. Pride of ownership was tempered by a touch of sadness: the woman who'd bought it new had been proud of this refrigerator once. But she and her family had lost everything when this frightful Depression ground them down.

This was the day Dorothea usually cleaned the Shelvador. But when she surveyed the interior she found the job already done. The condiments were lined up neatly on the door. The jars of pickles gleamed. She looked more closely. The shelves showed no smears nor were there puddles. Even the bottle of chilled water she kept was full. She didn't have to wonder long. Emma was really too much. While Dorothea was busy with her roomers, Emma had eaten her breakfast in the kitchen and then cleaned the refrigerator inside and out.

Dorothea shook her head. Soon the kitchen would be so bright she'd have to wear sunglasses like a Hollywood star. Smiling she went into the front room and got the Hoover vacuum from the closet. This room where the boarders congregated after supper was to be the big cleaning job today. If they finished and had some time before getting supper ready they would dust and vacuum the front stairway.

She looked around, Emma must be sweeping the front stoop. The girl was an energetic worker but she'd been out there long enough to clean an entire veranda.

Dorothea set the vacuum on the front room rug, plugged it in but didn't turn it on. Crossing the room to the front door, she had her hand on the knob when she heard voices outside.

Emma's voice was cheerful, bantering a little. "For sure, Denny? You saw a real buffalo? You ain 't telling me a tale?"

"There was a herd of them penned up. Touched one. Uncle Emmet works in Oklahoma, near Tulsa. Last summer I stayed with him. I can leave school this year and then I'm going to Oklahoma and work in the oil fields like Uncle Emmet," Denny, the bakery delivery boy, said.

"Work. I'd better get back to mine. Thanks, Denny, I got to go now."

"OK, Emma, I'll see you soon. OK?"

They laughed and their happiness, bright and light like the morning, rang out.

Dorothea hurried back to the vacuum. Emma entered carrying the broom; the door slammed behind her.

"Oh, sorry," she said. "That Denny from the bakery wanted to chat. I sent him on his way. But look." She held out a brown paper sack. "He brought two doughnuts. We can have them with coffee later if you want."

"That will be fine, dear. Put them in the kitchen and let's get started." Dorothea turned on the vacuum. Emma hurried to the kitchen and came back to the front room. She hummed as she used the feather duster on the tables and then on the piano. While Dorothea vacuumed Emma used the broom to sweep out the places too narrow for the Hoover.

As she vacuumed the rug Dorothea reflected on the last three days. The days weren't too cold yet, though at night the temperature was falling pretty low. It was September and the nights would get colder.

Dorothea and Preston had taken walks and spent as much time as possible together. He was comfortable to be around. However she'd sensed the increase in tension in him as the days wore on. This morning he'd been up early.

After breakfast before leaving he'd kissed her.

"Don't worry." He said. "It's likely I won't be back til late."

The heavy four-door, eight-cylinder De Soto bounced through one puddle and slithered into the next one. The auto chugged along; it wasn't like his Ford. Preston was confident that the green vehicle could get through all but the deepest wallow.

The sun warmed up the interior of the car so he took off his jacket and hat. His pistol was in the capacious glove box. The car slithered past the deformed tree where he'd met Pen. Another couple of miles to go and he was getting concerned that his plan might fail if he got stuck too soon.

He didn't have to worry. At a crossroads he heard the sound of a car motor struggling to start. The engine ground, caught, then died. He heard someone cursing. Fifty yards or so down the hidden side road he glimpsed the roofs of some buildings. Could it be that the mechanics were struggling with the engine of a black Packard?

The east side of the road was muddy but he could see car tracks going through the mess. On the west the water had puddled to form what appeared to be a deep bog.

He shifted the DeSoto into reverse, backed up and turned onto the side road. Once on the road he jerked the wheel to the left. The car slid into the water laboring to find traction. The tires ground on some rocks and leaped ahead and Preston thought his plan might fail. But there was no need for him to worry. The car settled and the tires spun.

The dark water reached nearly to the running board. He rolled up his trouser legs, took off his shoes and waded through the chill puddle. Beyond the mud pit he slipped on his shoes and crossed the road. He stopped in front of a pine cabin that was partially hidden by the surrounding trees. The place now appeared deserted. He stopped and called out. A boy of perhaps fourteen limped from behind the shanty and peered at Preston. A dog followed him, saw Preston and barked. Both boy and dog ran off.

As Preston approached the cabin he saw a large dilapidated barn to his left. Tall doors of the barn were almost closed. Beyond the house and barn was a low shed. In the brush next to the shed an old and rusted Ford was partially obscured.

From the barn the boy returned accompanied by a tall man. Preston recognized them as the pair he'd seen a few days ago.

The man said, "Hey, you, what you want? We got nothing

for sale."

Preston looked away and smiled blandly. The man facing him had a scar across his right cheek. "No, not looking for anything to buy. I'm a salesman. They told me in Lake Harbor that I could find a highway out this way that would take me south to Indiana. I'm from Indiana, going back home." He turned and pointed at the De Soto. "But now I'm lost and stuck. I need directions and somebody to pull me out. Can you help me?"

The man looked at Preston for a long moment, took off his cap, shook his grizzled head and frowned. "Naw, I don't think we can help you."

"But I could pay you." The unfriendly guy kept his dark gaze on Preston and his hands stuck deep into his jacket pocket.

"Uncle Del we got Tony and Sid." The boy said.

The tall man stared at the boy, his dark eyes never blinking. The boy winced and slowly turned away. "The boy don't know his place. Needs some more lessons. He hasn't learned yet that a big mouth can get him in deep trouble." He spread his long arms in a sarcastic invitation. "OK, Teddie, you so eager for more work. Go on, go get the damned horses and pull this fellow out of the mud." As the boy turned the scarred man kicked his leg. The cripple cried out and limped toward the barn.

Uncle Del turned back to Preston. "Mister you wait right here. The dummy will bring the horses. And you owe me two dollars. If you want someone to show you the highway that'll be another dollar. We ain't running no charity." He held out his hand. The final joint on his right little finger was missing. Preston gave the man three one-dollar bills.

Teddie led the horses out of the barn and they stood stolidly while the young man harnessed them and attached the singletree. Uncle Del watched for a moment and then went into the cabin.

As Teddie led the horses to the road two fellows wearing caps came out from the cabin. They watched Preston indolently while they smoked cigarettes. One of them wore his jacket over his shoulders and cradled his right arm with his left hand.

Preston walked next to Teddie along the road. The young man seemed friendly and to have suffered no serious damage from Uncle Del's boot.

"Tony get over, you bully." Teddie ordered the gray horse on the left. "If I let him he'll push Sid all the way over into the ditch." He said. "He's younger and thinks he's the boss. Sid's an old cuss, don't care about nothing but his evening oats."

"You've got a way with those animals."

"Thanks, mister. Me and my sister get along with animals. Pen, that's my sister, and me going to save our money and have a farm. Lots of animals." He concentrated and then announced, "We live in the shed behind the house. She's gone all day. Sells apples and such. Uncle Del tries to make her stay here, but she don't listen to him. She's got to be moving."

Teddie backed the horses through the mud to the car. He waded in and hooked the singletree to the front chassis of the DeSoto. He stepped back, called their names and ordered them to pull. The horses leaned into their harnesses and strained. The car rocked forward, but settled back.

Teddie allowed the animals a moment to rest and then shouted "Pull" again. This time they responded, muscles bulging. The muddy car came free.

"Tony, Sid, good horses," He patted their chests.

One of the men by the barn called out, "Teddie, give them a kiss." They laughed, ground out their cigarettes and went back into the barn.

Teddie turned to Preston with a smile. "Them horses got you loose, mister. That was a deep one but they got you out."

"Thanks. Those are good horses and you handle them well. Now the highway?"

"Sure, just turn around here on the dry part of the road and go back to the wider dirt road. Turn left that'll be east. Just stay on that to the paved road, turn right and that'll take you home."

"Thanks," he handed Teddie a dime, "that's for you." The boy thanked him and carefully put the coin in a leather pouch.

Preston wanted a last look at the homestead so he walked with Teddie back along the road opposite the cabin. Uncle Del was standing by door. "Stop yammering, dummy, get those animals back to the barn, there's work to be done."

The boy's smile disappeared as he hurried to the barn. Preston returned to his car.

On the drive to the highway Preston remembered the layout of the gang's hideout. With any luck he was sure the gang could be captured without a fight.

Preston laughed out loud. He'd be willing to bet that the curtains on the barn windows hid an expensive black Packard.

Chapter 28

Dorothea looked out her bedroom third floor window. Evening fog rolled eastward from Lake Michigan slowly engulfing the jetty north of the house. In the distance the foghorn repeated a two-note call, a forlorn caution. Just north of the rooming house the ship warning light flashed overhead barely penetrating the gathering grayness.

She turned from the window and looked at Preston sitting in the easy chair. Her eyes were sad. "That's impossible."

Preston had just burst into the room and embraced her. He'd sat, placed his clasped hands between his knees and said: "Dorothea, let's get married."

At the window she tried to clear the confusion she felt. She had to think clearly, be decisive while not hurting Preston or driving him away.

Not put off by her response he lit a cigarette and laughed. "We get along. Like the same things."

She shook her head. "We don't know each other at all. There's things about me that would shock you."

"Yeah, sure, you spoil the roomers. Me. I'm a real horror." He laughed and paced the room.

She watched him as he moved about nervously. She opened her mouth but before she could speak Preston laughed again.

"Sure, you're a spoiler." He sat for a moment and then was on his feet again. "This police work is for a young guy." He winced and massaged his hip. "I need to think about turning in my badge and collecting my pension. Being here with you has made up my mind."

"Preston, let's talk about this another time. OK?"

"Yeah, we'll talk again after me and Spivak have those crooks under lock and key. We're going to take that gang of car thieves tomorrow night. Wait until they're sleeping and then wham." His right fist hit his open left hand.

"You should be thinking about being careful. There'll be shooting won't there?"

"Nah, we'll be on them before they know what's happening. Still be in their pajamas with the sandman." He jumped up and took her in his arms. "Let's have a drink. Then we'll go to bed. I'll convince you that I'd be a good husband." She held him for a moment before doing what he asked.

తు   తు   తు

She woke and stretched. The fog had blown inland and the moon provided the only light in the room. She had an unclear memory of a noise. Had someone shouted? Was some one in trouble?

Preston groaned, rolled over and stretched his right arm over her. His warmth was inviting but it was time for her to be stirring.

That clock was no friend this morning. She had a slight headache from the gin and was tired from the lovemaking; getting up was a chore. She eased out from under his arm and put her bare feet on the cold floor.

While she washed her face at the basin she thought she heard something slam – a door? – then a short, sharp cry again. Was someone hurt? Had it come from Opal's house? Had Opal or Emma fallen?

She dressed in her work clothes of yesterday. If Emma had come to work early and fallen on the street or stairs in the dark, she'd tell her a thing or two. After she made sure she was all right. Dorothea found her shoes and hurried down the stairs through the front door and out onto the sidewalk where she stopped to listen. The fog dampened sounds.

She heard a dull thump. The noise had come from her friend's house.

"Hello? Is everything all right?" Opal's front door was open a bit. Dorothea pushed open the door and slowly entered.

Someone grabbed her arm, twisted it painfully and jerked her into the front room. She shrieked and struggled ineffectively as the hands forced her to the floor.

Opal struggled up from the floor. "You're the devil. Earl Duffy, you'll pay in hell." She lunged forward at the man holding Dorothea.

Dorothea's arm was twisted until she thought it would break. Earl cursed. "Ah, shut your gob, crone. I will not be denied what is mine."

Dorothea was driven to the floor by a blow to the back of her head. Her arm was released.

"Rascal," Opal cried out. "You've no right . . ." Her cries ended with the wet smack of flesh against flesh. Opal stumbled and sprawled to the floor.

The assailant stormed into the kitchen, knocking over a small table. "Where's the little bitch?" He announced furiously. "Stop sneaking about. You'll not get away from me."

Dorothea struggled to her feet and staggered across the room into the small kitchen behind Duffy. From the small box room off the kitchen Emma cried out. "Leave me be. Don't hurt me."

"Damn," Duffy cried out in pain. "Ah, I reckoned you for a she-cat. You'll be screeching soon." From the box room there were Earl's shouts and Emma weeping as she tried to fight. Dorothea made it across the kitchen and rested against the stove. Her hand found a heavy round object. She snatched up Opal's rolling pin and followed the sound of the girl's crying.

One small window silhouetted the man's massive shape above a small form. Dorothea raised the weapon and swung it with all her might. He yelled in pain. A counter blow to her chest took all her breath and she fell unconscious.

Another man was speaking now. Preston's voice, warning and authoritative. Earl's deep, gruff complaints rumbled in response and then Dorothea lost consciousness again.

When Preston began to lift her Dorothea struggled.

"Well, there she is, she's coming round. I thought she'd come up fighting." Preston said.

"Sure enough, she's a fighter."

Now sitting in a chair Dorothea was aware of two things. It was light outside and it was time to get breakfast started.

Her head hurt.

Preston knelt beside her and held her hand. "Do you want to go to the hospital, get checked over?"

"Hospital? Don't be foolish. Some strong coffee and break-fast will get us going." She rubbed her head. "Sergeant Spivak, what are you doing here?" She looked around slowly. "Where?"

"Take it easy, Dorothea. The whack that guy gave you shook up your memory a bit. It'll come back." Spivak puffed on his cigar as he stood by the door in Opal's house.

"Where is everybody?"

"Opal and Emma are over at your place, Dorothea. Knowing them, they're getting cleaned up and will have the coffee on."

"What happened, Preston?"

"According to Opal her brother-in-law Earl Duffy came here from Detroit meaning to get Emma, to make off with her. When Opal answered the door he hit her and shoved her back into the front room. When you got here he had been chasing Emma and had her trapped in that room off the kitchen and . . . well . . . it was pretty clear what he had planned. Your arrival interrupted him." Preston said.

"And he would have carried out his plans," Milton Spivak added, "if you hadn't come along."

Dorothea slowly recalled images of the fight, the noise and swearing. "I didn't do much. Got walloped a time or two that's all." She gently massaged the back of her head.

"Modest as well as beautiful," Preston said.

Then he said to Dorothea, "He had poor Emma trapped, was tearing at her clothes. And you went in and hit him with a rolling pin."

"Lord, about took his ear off you did." Spivak observed chuckling.

"Yeah, I got up just as you were going downstairs, heard the ruckus. Just in time to stop that brute." Preston patted the pistol in his pocket. "Earl knew I would shoot. Almost plugged him anyway after seeing him standing over you like that."

"Officer on patrol heard the noise, rang for help on the callbox and here I am." The sergeant finished. "Earl is in the lock-up now. May the surgeon sew that ear back to his head with a long, dull needle."

"Well, gentlemen," she stood up, "Come on, I think I owe you both breakfast."

Chapter 29

As Preston drove through the night, he and Spivak did not say much. Beyond the lumbering De Soto there was nothing visible through the darkness but an occasional road sign. They led a convoy of six cars carrying two-dozen deputies and city policemen to the homestead where the car thieves were holed up. Everything was ready. Spivak had a search warrant secure in his inside jacket pocket. Earlier Spivak briefed the police officers about the operation. Preston explained the layout of the homestead.

Nighttime and they'd steal up to the house and the barn getting as close to the structures as possible. At the sergeant's command they'd rush the hoodlums. Hopefully not a shot would be fired.

At the earlier meeting the sergeant had stated that there was to be no shooting unless he gave the order.

"We supposed to let these crooks get the first shot at us? We can't protect ourselves?" The protest came from Clint Nivens, the big sheriff's deputy called "Cowboy" by his colleagues. Preston met him previously in Spivak's office and wondered again whether Cowboy would follow orders.

"Well, Clint, if you're getting scared you can stay here and answer the phone." Spivak said as he stared down the deputy.

Clint Nivens dropped his gaze and silently endured the laughter of the men around him. Eyes glinting he'd fondled the Browning Automatic Rifle resting in his lap.

Were there a firefight to erupt all officers had been warned not to shoot at the small shack behind the house. Preston did not want Pen or Teddy hurt. Everything had been covered, contingencies discussed. Preston felt confident, excited but confident. He came to the turn-off and shut off the automobile lights. The cars behind him did the same. Preston did not need the headlights. He'd been down this road before.

The main dirt avenue would lead to a secondary one. Guided mainly by moonlight and driving slowly, Preston found the obscured road running past the hideout. He took a deep breath and checked the speedometer. No need to hurry. The longer the drive took the more likely the thieves would be sound asleep.

He let his mind wander again.

"Preston, you tell Dorothea" Spivak had told him yesterday, "that we'll keep that molester, Earl Duffy, locked up as long as possible. Since Opal and Emma don't want to bring formal charges, I'll have to let him out in a week to ten days. Wish I could do more."

"Milton you've been a good friend. We'll find some way to protect Emma from Duffy." Preston had tried to sound more assured than he felt.

Opal was a tough woman and had suffered no lasting effects from Duffy's blows. Physically Emma had also recovered but her aunt had told Dorothea that the young woman hadn't slept much since the attack.

∾ ∾ ∾

Using his spotlight now and again Preston eased the car along until he spotted his old tracks into the muddy slough. He swung the De Soto out into the road to give the car behind him clearance. A car with two officers slowly drove to the end of the road, beyond the cabin. Another auto would hang back and seal off the near end of the road. Preston waited as the tension rose.

"OK, Preston, let's do it," Spivak said. He drove past the slough and stopped opposite the cabin about twenty feet away. They got out of the vehicle and crept into the brush.

The undergrowth was denser than it appeared from the road. Feet tangled in sapling roots Preston fell hard and his impact set off barking from the shack. He heard confused shouting. Behind him Spivak yelled, "This is the police. You are surrounded. Come out with your hands up." He waited a few moments and called out again. "No need for anyone to get hurt. There's no chance of escape. Surrender."

A light in the house had blinked on. As Spivak yelled it went out.

"We'll never be taken alive, copper. Try and take us if you've any guts." A voice called out the challenge from the cabin.

After a moment of silence Preston saw the muzzle flashes from the cabin windows and the crack of their weapons. To his left there were flashes from the barn. Behind him Preston heard shouting. From the barn someone screamed, "I'm hit. Tommy, I'm wounded."

Preston shot at a muzzle blast from the cabin window. After the initial salvos there was silence. The barn was lit up from inside and a powerful engine roared. A Packard limousine burst through the barn doors headed for the police line and the road. Bullets hit the dark hood of the big car sparking into the night. The whine of ricochets filled the air like deadly insects. The windshield of the big auto exploded into fragments and smoke poured from the engine. The car ground to a halt halfway to the cabin. The driver's door was thrown open and a figure leaped out.

Behind him a desperate voice yelled. "Tommy. Don't leave me." Several pistol shots cracked, the BARs boomed and the man staggered a couple of steps and fell. All was quiet.

From a cabin window someone fired at Preston.

"Rotten coppers! I'll kill everyone of you cowards."

The BAR answered and there was silence.

"There. See that? Something ran into that shack. In the back there." A voice called out excitedly.

Preston shouted, "Don't shoot." His words were drowned out as heavy rifles roared. The shack quivered as the 30.06 rounds penetrated its thin pine walls. Preston screamed for them to stop, but it was too late.

From the other side of the clearing Spivak called out. "Surrender. Throw down your guns and come out into the light with your hands up."

The woods were quiet. There was faint whimpering somewhere. Spivak called out once more. Someone yelled and advised moving in. "Shut up," the sergeant ordered. "Everyone stay right where you are." Once again he ordered the mobsters to surrender. There was no answer.

"Preston?" Spivak called out. "You all right?"

"Yeah, Sergeant." He responded though his throat was dry and sore.

"Good. Got a flashlight?" Preston flashed it. "You take some men, move in and check things out. Be careful."

While Preston gathered three men, Spivak warned the others not to shoot. Preston sent two men to search the car and barn. He took one officer with him and went into the house.

In the two-room cabin there was the body of a middle age woman. She'd fallen on her stomach and her faded blue flannel nightdress was soaked with her blood. It looked as if she had tried to hide behind the wood stove. A revolver lay near her open hand.

He heard the steady dripping of something in the house. In the other room the man he knew as Uncle Del lay on his back in a pool of blood, a pistol clenched in his hand.

Preston left the deputy to collect the weapons and search the bodies. Outside Spivak ordered the car headlights to be turned on, trained on the homestead.. Preston walked out into the intense illumination.

A voice announced from the smoking Packard, "These two are deader than doornails." Another voice was choked, "God, what a mess."

A young constable came up and remembered to wipe away the tears on his face. "Sir," he said, "two horses are down in the barn. Still breathing but they're both gut shot."

Preston looked at him. The young fellow seemed more affected by the wounded animals than the dead men.

"Put them out of their misery," he said.

Preston holstered his pistol and walked away from the sounds of the investigation toward the shack. He winced as he heard two shots. He did not want to look into the splintered shack but knew he had to.

Preston pushed back the door and found that the dog's body had held it shut. The animal had been trying to get to the youngsters and the movement must have drawn the gunfire. Just beyond the canine corpse there was the boy Teddie on his back. Shot through both lungs Teddie's body arched sharply, a low moan came from his bloody mouth. As Preston watched the boy regurgitated a gout of blood and died.

Beyond Teddie, Pen lay still beneath a rough table. She too was on her back. The bullets from the automatic rifles had blown her face away. On her dress the medal he'd given her glinted in the thin illumination of his flashlight. In the corner a red poppy blossom stood upright in her straw hat.

He left the shack and stumbled through the heavy vegetation. Weeds and saplings tripped him and tore at his jacket. At the edge of the road he came upon a group of officers laughing and smoking cigarettes by an automobile.

Taller than the others, Clint Nivens fondled his rifle as he laughed and took a drink from a pint bottle of whiskey.

Preston snatched the weapon from him and bashed the barrel against a tree.

"Hey," Nivens yelled in protest and tried to wrench the rifle from his grasp. Preston dropped the rifle and knocked him down.

Preston did not recall taking his pistol from the holster nor cocking the weapon. He raised the pistol to Niven's forehead.

"No, don't do it. Please?" Nivens begged.

Preston lowered his weapon. The deputy scrambled to his feet as Preston lurched into the shadows.

Chapter 30

"Thanks." Dorothea accepted the headache powder nestled in the white, pudgy hand of Mordechai McNeil.

He's trying to be helpful, she reminded herself. Still she had a hard time relaxing when the round little man was peering at her.

"You must take care of yourself, Dorothea. We all rely on you," he said with a little bow. "Please take care of yourself." He turned and left the house. She forced herself to smile at him and went back to dusting the front room.

Later in the kitchen in the midst of the post-dinner cleanup she remembered the medicine and took it with a glass of water. By the time she and Emma were through with the dishes the pain above her eyes had lessened.

She sent Emma home and climbed the stairs. In her room she didn't bother turning on the lights. After a moment of blessed rest stretched out on the bed, she got up. Her work dress might do for another day. If she fell asleep in it there would be wrinkles.

In her nightgown under the covers she wished Preston were here to hold her. It had been two days since she'd seen him; three days since Spivak came by to recount to her the bloody shootout.

"We found those youngsters shot dead. Poor things."

Spivak said. "There was no sign of Preston. He'd scared the bejesus out of some of the deputies and then disappeared. They thought he was out of his mind, was going to shoot them. Dorothea, you see him tell him to get in touch, will you?"

She had agreed and then waited for a call that didn't come. That Preston was a troublesome devil, she decided. She worried about him but there was no way that she would go out into the cold night to look for the man. He was a grownup and could take care of himself. If his fondness for drink was ruling him and he was drunk somewhere, she prayed he was safe. Whatever his weaknesses Preston was a good man.

She had expected that when she reached her forties she would be finished with romantic foolishness. She'd almost reached that mark but Preston had come along. She wondered if that was a blessing or curse as she slipped into sleep.

In the middle of the night Dorothea was startled awake. Had she called out his name? Her back ached and the headache had returned. She got out of bed, crossed the cold room to the cabinet and poured a small drink of gin. Easing into her chair, she sipped the liquor. It helped.

The lakeshore beacon flooded the room for a moment. The light was followed by the foghorn's sad, penetrating note. She got up and went to the window. Wraiths of fog drifted inland over the dunes. The snow had stopped. Shivering, Dorothea donned her robe and returned to the chair. She took another drink.

Preston had told her about Pen, the little girl who had lived among the abandoned farms and sold apples. He'd said that he'd given Pen the religious medal his daughter had given him.

Dorothea's daughter had died, too.

She handled the recurring pain of the loss by imagining the name she might have given the child. What would she have named her little girl?

A young woman thrilled with her newly discovered pregnancy and sure she'd live with her first lover forever, she'd picked the name Priscilla for her child-to-be. For Dorothea, the name signified permanence, hope.

The baby died and the father left her. Priscilla became a name linked with naiveté and gullibility.

Years later she thought the baby would have been an Emily. Dorothea liked the old fashioned, straitlaced, strong sound of Emily. That daughter would have been confident, self-sufficient. The name seemed to give the never-daughter substance.

Now she decided she would have named the daughter never-to-be Ann. Simple, decisive, a survivor for sure, like her never-to-be mother. Mother and daughter would have been great friends.

Dorothea finished the gin and placed the glass on the table. A dog barked. The deep sound, almost a howl, came again from farther away as if the animal were lost. She wept for her never-to-be daughter and for her lost Preston.

To be hung over and waiting for the bar to open was hell. Smoking a cigarette at least took his attention from the nausea for a moment. Tobacco smoke curled up and dissipated, diffusing into the cold, humid air.

His clothes were still damp and clammy from being out in

the snow last night. He'd run away from, what was the word? A charnel house: a place of dead bodies and bones. How long ago had it been? It was three days and the image of Pen and Teddie dead was as clear in his mind as if he'd just seen it.

He couldn't get that place out of his mind.

He didn't owe anybody anything.

His throat spasmed and he gasped with the pent up tears. Could he remember how to cry? Sadness was like a great pressure inside. Still the tears wouldn't come. Why bother? He sat up in the front seat of the Ford the steering wheel pressed against his stomach. He'd fled the police station leaving the DeSoto and taking the state police Ford.

No matter how hard he stared at the face of his wristwatch he couldn't see the hands. It felt like it must be early in the morning. After rubbing his eyes on his jacket sleeve he was able to focus, see the hands and make out the time. It was almost 6 A.M. When would this tavern open?

Those kids, Pen and Teddie, had been blown apart like worthless garbage. Paper targets, that's all. Stop it. He shouldn't be thinking about that. The image of the medal and the red flower flared into his aching head. Now Preston cried. The deep, wrenching sobs hurt his chest. His heart threatened to burst. He forced himself to stop. Wiped his face on his sleeve.

Damn tavern wouldn't open. He punched the car window in frustration and the pain in his knuckles shocked him. Head resting on the wheel, he cradled his bruised hand and dozed.

Last night he'd been at Hardy's. The place was dangerous for him and that's why he went there. He hoped some criminals would assume that since he was drunk, he'd be an easy one to roll.

Even better perhaps some hoodlum would remember he was a cop. No one had paid any attention to him. He got falling down drunk. When he left Hardy's it was snowing.

Somehow he'd driven to another place to drink, closer to the docks, smaller, rougher. There drinks until his memory became blank. He'd slept in the Ford. Now he peered at the painted sign above the bar door identifying it as "The Bell."

The sound of a metal drum being dragged through the bar door informed him that he might soon get a drink. Stumpy, an ill-tempered man he recalled vaguely from last night rolled a trash barrel across the sidewalk and left it at the curb.

Preston's hands quivered. He watched them shake and knew that he wasn't far from sickness. The doctor in the sanitarium had told him that delirium tremens occurred when there was extreme alcohol poisoning followed by abrupt abstinence. He'd better get a drink soon or he'd be seeing snakes slithering along the cold sidewalks. They'd try to bite him. Just like before at the sanitarium. He got out of the car, ran his fingers through his hair and smoothed his wrinkled jacket. Concentrating, he slowly stepped to the tavern door and went in.

"Come for breakfast, have you?" Stumpy the bartender, an old man with a limp and a left arm missing a hand and half a forearm sneered a greeting. He did not stop energetically sweeping the floor broom clasped to his chest with the left stump. Preston sat in a rickety chair and looked up to see the barkeep peering at him.

"Getting sick, are you? Need a drink real bad?" Stumpy said and turned back to sweeping.

In the long, dim room wooden unpainted tables were

scattered about. Unmatched wooden chairs sat by each of the tables. In a corner in the rear behind a long table that served as a bar Stumpy rested the broom and busied himself rinsing glasses in a sink. "What'll it be, Mister Preston?"

"Double shot and a beer, Stumpy. And be quick will you?" He had to be careful. Stumpy had the real power and could torture him by taking his time. He dug in his pockets and found a couple of crumpled bills he threw on the table. Searching his jacket pockets he found a pack of cigarettes and lit one.

"I try to be fast with the orders, Mister Preston. I can only do so much being as cripple and all." The bartender's whine accompanied the clunk of a beer bottle on the table. Preston watched the amber whiskey pour from the bottle into a glass. Preston snatched up the liquor and drank it in one gulp. The cheap liquor burned his raw throat. His eyes watered, his stomach clenched trying to reject the fiery liquid.

With a struggle the drink stayed down. He sighed and took a deep drag on his cigarette. He drank from the beer bottle; the liquid cooled and soothed his throat. He waved the shot glass at Stumpy. "Another," he gasped.

One more drink and he felt better. Life was possible. His nerves relaxed and his hands no longer shook. Eyes grew heavy.

"May I buy you a drink, sir?"

Preston roused and tried to focus on the round sleek face. He nodded.

Mordechai McNeil gestured at Stumpy and then said, "Excuse me for interrupting your reverie. Might we talk?"

The drinks arrived and Mordechai lit cigarettes for them. A diffident little finger extended, he sipped his whiskey and made a face. "My word that whiskey is raw, isn't it?"

He pushed the glass back and leaned close. "I must confess that I have not been entirely candid with you, sir." Mordechai blew out smoke and watched it curl in the air. "I do travel and sell, but in addition to my retail work I do favors for people. Of course, they show their appreciation financially."

Preston finished his drink and wondered what he was talking about.

"I do private investigations for families and their surrogates —attorneys and insurance companies." He slid his chair closer to the table. "Are you familiar with any of these names: Alma Dundee, Max Volstad or Clement Schulz?"

Preston shook his head, unable to concentrate..

"No matter. All the people I've named have several things in common. First, they are elderly and not in good health. Second, they are not to be found. Third, each received a monthly stipend from a pension or family funds."

Preston wished the story was over and that his glass was filled again.

"One more commonality." He hesitated and smiled. "Their benefits are still being paid, mailed to their last known address. Care to guess what address that is?"

"I have a headache and have never been good at games," Preston mumbled.

"So sorry. Perhaps another drink would alleviate the pain." He motioned for Stumpy. "The checks are sent to Miss Dorothea Dolan's address. The checks are endorsed by people who no longer reside there and who may no longer be alive."

Part Three

November 1940

Chapter 31

Dorothea shivered and pulled the sweater more tightly about her. The only room in this damned barn of a house that's warm is my lonely kitchen. She sipped some coffee. Setting down her cup she slopped some onto the table. "Damn," she shouted. Surprisingly tears prickled at the corners of her eyes.

"What the hell is going on?" She protested impatiently but she knew the answer to the question. She was feeling sorry for herself. House cold. Weather miserable. And she was alone, cold inside and out.

Tears forgotten, she recalled Opal's shrill cry of disbelief just a week ago.

"You'd do that for us? What happens if we get sick and can't pay you back?" They were standing in the kitchen. Emma too had heard Dorothea's offer to pay the train fair to California for the two of them. The offer had caused Emma to sit down and cover her face.

"Well, I'm ready to take a chance if you are, Opal. That Duffy is due to get out soon. You want to take a chance on him returning?"

Opal agreed to the journey when Dorothea offered to watch Opal's house. Were they to get established, using contacts

Dorothea gave them, the house would be sold.

"Could use the money to pay you back," Opal said.

After all of them had hugged and cried, Dorothea sent them off. "You get ready. Take what you need and close up the house. Make sure you stay healthy and have a happy life."

It was cold again today and she had no one to talk to. Preston might be frozen in a ditch somewhere. He'd been gone almost three weeks. Not a note or a phone call in all that time. The rat. Why couldn't he just come on home and let her take care of him? Men were so hard to figure out. Finally get a good one and he disappears. She wiped her moist cheeks and looked out the window at the few snowflakes blowing about in the chill morning.

The first week after Preston disappeared Milton Spivak had come by to find out how she was doing. There hadn't been a visit from him in a while.

Last week a brusque fellow named Anderson had called from Grand Rapids. Without any manners, he'd accused her of obstructing justice. Dorothea had told him to go to hell and hung up.

But she was still worried that her treatment of Anderson might get Preston in trouble. How could he get into more trouble?

She sipped more coffee and very carefully set the cup down. She groaned as she rubbed her back. There was time enough to rest for a bit. Breakfast had been served and the roomers were gone. The kitchen was cleaned up. Preparing supper could be put off until early afternoon. She would fry potatoes and onions with drippings saved from a roast.

Now she had a little time for herself and all she could do was sit in the kitchen and drink bitter, reheated coffee. These days she had no help. She had to do all the cooking, and cleaning herself. She was tired all the time. Emma had spoiled her. This whining had to stop. There was food and shelter. Lots of people didn't even have the essentials. Under just about any railway bridge there were poor devils barely surviving.

Without any notice Mordechai McNeil disappeared. She'd never felt close to that one. It seemed to her he was always standing around watching the others. Still she did wonder what became of him. The other day she'd packed his things and put them in the storage room. He was creepy sure enough, but he did pay for his room and board promptly.

That left her with only three paying guests: Nils Nilson, Beryl Richards and Minnie Quinton. Rent from three rooms would not pay her overhead. Her savings would keep things going for a few months but she'd eventually lose her business. Things got even worse when Nils left for New York where he hoped to get some news of his brother. There had been only one resort left her.

She'd fed the two women living with her and then dressed up and gone out. Tired but camouflaging her weariness with a forced gayness, she'd started going to Hardy's tavern. She'd done it before.

In the rough drinking crowd she knew she would attract men. Rootless males with no place to stay would soon learn that Dorothea was a businesswoman. She sent the lecherous and the impecunious on their ways and recruited potential roomers.

The wearisome evenings had paid off and she'd saved her rooming house. Now Phil Riley and Tom Duncan two loud, fun-loving Irishmen had moved in. Later little Franklin Anders had limped to her door, a near invalid, and rented a room. Her business had survived.

Last night it had been particularly hard to fall asleep. Where had Preston gone? In her heart she felt he was still alive. She wanted to comfort him, hold him close and tell him that the terrible occurrences in the shootout had not been his fault.

~ ~ ~

The doorbell startled her. It took Dorothea several moments to figure out where she was. It was bright daylight and she'd fallen asleep in her chair in the kitchen. The doorbell rang again.

Rising from the chair she trudged the distance to the front door. The peephole revealed the nervous, slender form of Sergeant Milton Spivak. Holding the heavy door open she welcomed the policeman into the house out of the cold wind.

Spivak pulled off his hat and smiled. Her old friend looked tired and worried. Still half-asleep she waited for him to speak.

He shook the drops of moisture from his fedora and did not look at her. "No time to beat around the bush. Dorothea this is going to sound crazy, like I'm prying maybe. But how close were you and Preston, you know, more than roomer and landlady?"

At the question the cobwebs left by sleep disappeared, "Why shame on you. Listening to rumors and gossip, are you?" Why was she being coy? What difference could it make now to admit they had been lovers?

He blushed but went on with his strange questions. "If you and Preston were, you know, more than friends get your coat on, come with me. I'll fill you in later. No questions now I don't have much time." He moved to the door and waited.

Still perplexed Dorothea went to the front hall closet for her coat. She stepped into galoshes. Standing up she nodded to the policeman and followed him out.

Spivak drove his own car, an old Ford four-door. The policeman steered carefully over wet streets through the morning traffic. The department store and the five-and-ten were both putting up Christmas decorations though it was more than a month before the holiday. At first she looked out the window at the passing scenes trying to get her head working properly. Soon she recognized the neighborhood around the Lake Harbor Hospital.

Had someone been hurt? Heavens, had Preston been found? Was he alive? Would she have to identify his body? If he were alive, no matter how sick, she'd care for him.

She forced her silent speculations to stop. The car slowed in front of the large white hospital building. Spivak drove slowly through the parking lot to the one story charity wing partially hidden by the main hospital building and a grove of white pines. He parked, turned off the motor and turned toward Dorothea.

"Sorry about the secrecy. You'll see in a moment why I had to keep it quiet." Spivak stopped speaking and looked down and wiped his forehead. "If the police chief or the state police ever found out about me withholding information I'd be out of a job. And Preston would be in jail." He nodded toward the hospital. "Preston Duhamel is inside. He's listed as John Doe. They don't know who he is."

He waited for the news to sink in. "Preston about drank himself to death. He turned in his gun and car to me and sent a telegram to Grand Rapids resigning. Anderson claims Preston has broken some laws by getting drunk on duty and not returning the car and gun to him. He wants him called up in front of a judge. That'd be the end of Preston for sure. Cops don't last long in prison."

"One of my boys found him in an alley down by the docks. I didn't know what to do then I remembered Noah Pflam told me once about you two. That's why I took this chance."

A wan smile creased his narrow face. "He's in there. I owe him but I got to be careful. I've got a family."

She took hold of his arm and squeezed it. "No more, I'll take care of him."

"Thanks. He's not in very good shape. I guess he's been living on a mainly liquid diet ever since the shoot-out in August."

"Oh, poor man," she whispered.

"He has nowhere to go." He took her hand. "The doctor says he's pretty sick."

"Let me go to him, Milt."

He nodded and she got out of the car. She started toward the building but came back.

"No need to wait for me. I'll get a taxi. I'll stay with him for a while."

As she walked alone into the charity ward Dorothea steeled herself for what she might see. Inside there was a single long room with a low ceiling. Rows of beds, heads to the wall, and all occupied by men, were against the long walls leaving a wide aisle down the middle. In the center was the high desk of the nurse's station.

A squad of young women dressed in white uniforms clustered about some beds at the far end of the room. Two older women in blue uniform dresses mopped the tiled floor.

The echoing space was filled with the low-pitched cacophony of suffering. Men moaned, coughed, cursed, complained, emitting sounds that rebounded from the institutional beige walls. Dorothea fought the urge to put her hands over her ears as she looked about wondering how to proceed.

She moved into the room toward the nurse's station. Beneath the dense odor of disinfectant there was the stink of unclean bodies, infection and excrement.

"Visiting hours in the afternoon, 4 to 6. We have work to do." Dorothea had not noticed the thin-lipped nurse clad in a crackling white uniform, white hat firmly pinned to her short gray hair. She held a clipboard against her bosom as if it were armor.

"My brother was just brought in." Dorothea smoothly improvised. She looked into the nurse's cold blue eyes and smiled humbly. "They told me he might be dying."

"What's your name?" The nurse looked through the pages on her clipboard.

"Please, ma'am, he's here as John Doe."

"Aha, we have four of those. Brought in by the police, all of them with alcohol poisoning." She concluded with a judgmental sniff.

"I just want to sit with him, nurse. I'll help care for him."

"You mustn't interfere. The John Does are the four beds in the far corner on the left. Perhaps you'll be able to recognize him." Her sharp pencil was poised above a record sheet. "What is your name?"

Her name earned her free passage past the nurse's station.

Dorothea went to the corner and looked over the beds. One man rose up on his elbow and surveyed her.

"Hi, baby, you bring a bottle?" He laughed until he fell back coughing.

Two of the John Does were old and gray. The one who had flirted with her had red hair. The fourth man had a head of black hair with streaks of gray and a beard that contrasted with the white pillow. A bandage covered the left side of his face. He was the one she sought.

Preston lay on his back eyes shut, arms at his side and did not respond when she whispered his name. "Preston." She called out his name a little louder. "Preston." His eyes opened slowly.

Chapter 32

His eyes closed again. Through the afternoon Preston lay unmoving on the narrow iron hospital bed showing little response to the world around him. Dorothea sat next to him on a wooden chair and dozed, rousing only when a young nurse with detached efficiency administered a pill.

After hurrying to the rooming house to prepare supper, Dorothea returned and sat by Preston until she was made to leave in the evening.

On the second morning he was agitated. His eyes opened and looked about fearfully. Dorothea took his dry, cold hand in hers and he seemed to relax.

In the afternoon after taking a few sips of the thin broth for lunch he was again restless. She was jerked from her shallow sleep when he sat up. Arms waving, body shaking, he cried out in disjointed phrases.

"No firing. Please, don't anybody shoot."

"Apples. Apples? I'll take some."

"I'll protect you."

The patients near him muttered resentfully. One yelled, "Shut up."

When the episode ended he flopped back onto the pillow exhausted. Dorothea was busy soothing Preston's flushed face with a cool, moist cloth and did not hear the head nurse approach.

"He has had an extreme alcoholic shock to his brain. He came very close to dying," head nurse Flint said. "Sometimes patients this ill never recover. You must prepare yourself for that possibility."

Dorothea nodded and sat down again.

She came every day to wash him and urge him to eat. The wound on his cheekbone slowly healed.

Another day he sat up in bed, growling like a mad dog. Face distorted, he snarled at the emptiness at the foot of his bed, "You won't hurt her. I'll knock that smile off your fat face." Only with the help of some nurses was Dorothea able to prevent him from hurling himself from the bed.

Panting and sweating, Preston struck the mattress again and again until he fainted. After making sure he was breathing regularly, Dorothea stepped back and bumped into Nurse Flint.

Her lips were pressed into a thin line and her white-clad arms were crossed at her breast. "The doctor has witnessed these rages. He called them re-experiencing episodes. Some terrible experience your brother experienced is being relived in his mind. Only time and care might alleviate the condition. It would be best to care for him at home. In two days we require his bed. You must make other arrangements."

"Yes, Nurse Flint, I'll see to it." Dorothea nodded and sat beside the bed.

"Preston, dear," she whispered stroking his hand. "Soon you'll be home where you belong."

He abruptly awakened and looked at her, then around at the ward. "Where am I?"

"You are in the hospital."

"Am I sick?"

"Yes, dear, you are sick."

"Will I die?"

"I don't think you will."

He looked at Dorothea his brow wrinkled in concentration.

"Who are you?"

He was unconscious again before she could answer.

While he slept Dorothea considered plans to bring him back to the rooming house. She wanted to protect him from those who might hurt him like that jerk Anderson in Grand Rapids.

Only Beryl and Minnie had been with her when Preston lived there. But they cared little about the world around them. Minnie seldom played the piano anymore. The two old ladies spent their hours whispering to each other. Holding hands they toured the stores giggling at the new clothing styles draped on mannequins.

Max Volstad and Alma Dundee were gone. Clement had been removed from his pain. Nils Nilsson was in New York City trying to help his brother. Mordechai McNeil had disappeared. She'd packed away his clothes in a trunk in the storeroom.

Her present boarders, Phil Riley, Tom Duncan and the frail Franklin Kelly, had moved in while Preston had been on his binge. She'd bring him home under the same alias she used for him in the hospital. He'd be John Dolan, her brother.

Earlier Nurse Flint had told Dorothea that the clothes he'd

been wearing when admitted to the ward had been burned. So at home that evening she picked through the clothes left by Preston and found a dark suit, a blue shirt and a broad brimmed fedora. He'd need a heavy overcoat. She'd go over to the church resale shop where she could probably find one.

She readied the house for his return. Enlisting the help of Tom and Phil, the youngest and strongest of her guests the storage space next to her apartment was cleaned and a bed set up. The guests were told that Dorothea's brother had been ill and she would care for him.

On a sunny but cold day when the sky was gloriously blue and the lake a distant mutter Preston and Dorothea left the hospital in a cab. On the trip to the rooming house Preston roused and began calling out.

"Edith," he yelled, "listen to me. You are wrong. Just listen."

The taxi driver looked back at them anxiously. In response Dorothea smiled and stroked Preston's hand. He was silent, his eyes closed.

Not far from the house he roused again. Now his voice was soft and cajoling. "Solange, cherie, be careful at those busy streets, look both ways." Preston smiled and touched his neck. "Thank you for the medal. St. Christopher will protect me, I am sure." Still smiling he held his hand as if he were clasping a small fingers. "When you get home I'll take you for a drive. You'll meet Pen and Teddie, new friends of mine, you'll like them."

When the cab pulled up in front of Dorothea's house he was weakly calling out for Pen and Teddie.

"Miss Dolan, just stand aside and let us help the poor man." Phil said as he reached in to the back seat and eased Preston out of the car. Phil and the quiet Tom held Preston between them. Dorothea carried the small bag holding his belongings. The men did not have much trouble carrying Preston up the stairs. He'd lost so much weight. In the room, warm under the blankets, she hoped he'd rest.

"Thank you," she said to Phil and Tom, who were tiptoeing around trying not to wake the patient. "You fellows can go along. I'll take care of him." She handed them each a quarter. "Now you take this. You boys get yourselves a nice lunch before you go into work. Thanks for the help."

"You're certainly welcome, missus." Phil shook the coins in his big hand. "Tom, my boy, its some suds we'll be having." The young men clattered down the stairs and out the front door.

This evening for their supper she would bake a yellow cake and top it with boiled chocolate icing. It was their favorite.

In the quiet room she kissed Preston's unshaven cheek. Her heart seemed to swell painfully.

Oh, dear Preston, you are so hard on yourself. You end up carrying all the disappointments and sins of the world on your shoulders. I guess we are alike, you and me. Get well, I need you. Maybe we can learn to hold each other up.

Leaving the door open, she hurried downstairs. She had her house to run.

Throughout the rest of the day in the midst of her work Dorothea stopped and listened. Was he in pain, did he need her? Sometimes she'd run up the stairs and look in on him. His pale, unmoving face against the pillow looked like a statue or a death mask. She waited holding her breath until she saw the covers rise and fall. Reassured that he was resting, it was possible to return to her work.

After supper she took a bowl of broth and some buttered bread up to the third floor. She roused him, cooled the broth and spooned it into his mouth. He swallowed and peered at her.

"Dorothea, pretty as ever. Thank you, dear." The spoon rattled against the bowl. While she breathed deeply two tears moistened her blouse. Recovered she fed him some more soup.

When he had had enough broth she set aside the bowl and they held hands while the room grew dark. Preston's deep breathing and limp fingers told her he was asleep. Dorothea went to her bed. Please God, she prayed in the dark. Help him control his drinking. Help him to be able to take an occasional one and not overdo it. I'll love him, God, and take his mind off those terrible things that drove him to the liquor this time. Just show me how to help him. I can do it.

Preston recovered slowly. The fears and rages that tortured him came less often. His appetite remained weak and sporadic though he'd eat a little if Dorothea badgered.

Preston had been home about a week when Dorothea smelled alcohol on his breath. Checking, she found that the level in her gin bottle had gone down. She resolved to say nothing as long as his imbibing did not get out of control and threaten his health again.

"Preston, why don't you come down to the kitchen with me? I could use some help and I'd like your company." Since he's well enough to go to my room and find the gin, I'll put him to work, Dorothea resolved. In the kitchen with me there's less tempta-tion and opportunity. Perhaps sharing the work with her, and the nearness to the savory smells in the kitchen would strengthen his appetite.

"I don't know if I can help you much." His reply was slow as if he had to find each word before he uttered it.

"That's all right. Just come down and do what you can. When you're tired you can rest on the sofa in the front room."

"I'll give it a try." He dressed slowly in the mornings and sometimes buttoned his shirt crookedly. Once he forgot to put on his socks. Dorothea waited patiently helping when she could.

One day while she was slicing cheese to melt with the macaroni there was a sharp noise behind her. Preston was at his old place at the sink washing dishes. He'd dropped a plate.

As she watched he grunted and slowly bent over to pick up the pieces. Dorothea controlled the urge to hug him and returned to her task.

She looked at him again. He was on his hands and knees pushing the shards about. She knelt beside him.

"This way, Preston. This is how you can pick up the pieces. Be careful of the sharp edges."

Chapter 33

On a Monday morning from where she stood in the kitchen buttering slices of toast, Dorothea could see the quiet dark waters of Lake Michigan. Last night awakened by a winter storm she'd gotten up to look in on Preston. He was sleeping peacefully. Back in her room at the window looking out onto the lake and beach she'd watched the wind lashing the waters, the whitecaps exploding onto the beach.

Now it seemed as if the lake was exhausted by last night's exertions. There was scarcely a whitecap wave as the fishing boats headed out to begin their work. But she knew that Lake Michigan was resting, preparing for the next winter storm.

Dorothea shivered and pulled her sweater about her as she picked up the plate of toast. This winter had been a strange one so far. The air was always chill, but there hadn't been much snow.

She carried the toast into the dining room.

"Ah, that Tom," Phil stood up grinning and pointed at his friend. "Still waters and all. It's the quiet ones you must watch out for."

To her right Franklin Kelly took a slice and passed the plate to Beryl. On Dorothea's left at the end of the table Preston was sitting quietly, slowly stirring his cup of cold coffee. She wished he would eat something; he was so thin.

"I knew it was coming. Fellow bracing Tom would not shut his gob. Well, my friend smiled and popped him one. Put his lights out," Phil concluded.

Beryl emitted a nervous sound, "I'm sure Minnie and I don't agree with scuffling." Minnie nodded.

"Ah, miss," Phil said with a laugh and bow. "There was no scuffling. Tom simply put him to sleep." After the young men laughed, the room grew quiet as they finished the pile of toast Dorothea had provided.

Dorothea yawned and wished she could crawl back under the covers for an hour or two. A glance at Preston and she forgot about getting more sleep. It would be nice to be under the covers with him. He didn't respond when she patted his shoulder. Poor guy, he was having a tough time.

The radio broadcast the morning reports. There wasn't much new information. Employment had risen a little but the main economic indicators showed the country was not yet out of the depression. After the commercials the station played popular music. Bing Crosby sang his latest hit "Brother, Can You Spare a Dime?" Dorothea listened as the lyrics told of a man who'd helped build a railroad and had a dream. Why, the words went on, should that man "be standing in line just waiting for bread?" Dorothea felt a catch in her chest as the refrain summed up the loss of hope felt by the worker become panhandler: "Brother, can you spare a dime?"

The younger men, Phil, and Tom bickered about politics until Phil pointed at the Big Ben clock on the table. "Goldang, we be late for sure."

The warning resulted in a scramble by the two young

men for their jackets. The front door slammed shut behind them. Beryl and Minnie smiled staidly at the rush and then rose quietly. Franklin Kelly finished his bit of toast diffidently and limped up the stairs to his room.

Dorothea got up and, as she gathered the utensils, Preston roused from his revery and slowly stacked plates.

Working with Preston in the kitchen in the following days she observed that he still had no appetite and that he often seemed distant and preoccupied. Maybe he'd been taken off alcohol too quickly she reasoned. Perhaps if they had a little drink before bedtime he might perk up and eat more.

After helping him into his pajamas one night she took his arm and led him to her bedroom. As he sat in the chair staring off into space, she got the gin bottle down from the cabinet. "Let's have a drink."

The bottle held his gaze as he licked his lips. "Dorothea, I don't think I'd better. I think I should stay away from that stuff."

"Nonsense. You can handle it. You're recovered."

Anxious to show her trust she poured a bit of clear liquid into two glasses. "We worked hard today." She raised her glass. "Come on, Preston, it'll help us sleep."

They sipped and chatted. Preston seemed more alert. That night they slept together. Though they were chaste, the warmth and closeness was pleasant.

Drinking, however, had only a temporary beneficial effect. In the following days Preston again grew distant though she plied him with drinks. It seemed to Dorothea that there was a slight improvement in his eating.

When there was a break in the work Preston donned his coat and went onto the back porch. Though the air was cold and the wind blustery he sat in an old wooden chair and stared at the waters while he smoked.

"Preston, you'll catch a cold," she warned. She stopped him one day after breakfast as he headed out the back door. He looked at her blankly for a moment, then opened the door and went to his chair. That evening she swept the chair brushing off the bits of snow and ice adhering to it. She found an old cushion and tied it to the chair seat. The next time he went to the door she stopped him.

"Dear, you really must take this blanket. Drape it over your knees so you don't get sick." When he hesitated she insisted and he capitulated.

To Dorothea it seemed that Preston was still worrying about the past. He was trapped in dark memories. Was there something she could say, some dish she might cook? Within the limits of her tight budget she bought him treats. But the special coffee and the bakery cakes did not raise his spirits.

Late one morning when the wind gusted from the west and waves again dashed against the beach. Dorothea was reading the cartoon strips, the "funnies", in an old issue of the Lake Harbor Tribune. Smiling at the antics of the Katzenjammer Kids and Popeye, and sympathizing with the romantic difficulties of Mary Worth's friends, Dorothea heard distant shouts.

She saw Preston in his usual seat watching a group of children on their way home from school. They yelled and ran along the beach laughing and playing tag with the spray from the waves. She opened the door to the porch and went out into the bright winter sun. He didn't jump when she squeezed his shoulder.

"It wasn't your fault." She knew her words wouldn't ease him much but she had to try. Slowly his tired eyes moved from the children to meet hers. He nodded and his gaze was bleak. With a grunt he rose and went back into the house.

That evening after dinner Dorothea sat at the table alone. In the front room Phil, Tom and Franklin Kelly discussed politics as usual. She had tried to chat with Preston but he had responded with grunts and left the table to go up to his room. The bell from the front door penetrated her worried thoughts.

Phil answered the door, "For you, missus."

She crossed the room to the open front door and her heart skipped a beat. "Why Sgt. Spivak, is that you? Come on in." He entered the room revealing another figure, in uniform, behind him. "Who've you brought with you? It's Noah Pflam. What a nice surprise." She gestured for the two men to enter and led the way into the dining room.

Though both men had had breakfast at her table, the shock of seeing them together, looking serious and official, scared her. Had Preston done something that had brought the policemen on official business? Had she somehow been careless as she helped Clement?

"Dorothea, it's good to see you. Excuse us but we need to talk to Preston." Part of her fear dissipated.

They sat while she got cups and a pot of coffee. "You need privacy, Milton?" She felt she must stay close to Preston to protect him.

"No, Dorothea, you stay. We need a word with you as well."

She sent Tom up to tell Preston to come down. Phil followed him up the stairs.

After their cups were filled, Dorothea sat down and tried to smile. "You're both looking glum so I guess the news isn't good." Noah Pflam remained silent but fidgeted uncomfortably. He took a sip of coffee and smiled uncertainly.

Milton Spivak answered. "Well, Dorothea, I wouldn't say the news is all bad though it is – you might say – mixed."

"Mixed news did you say?" Preston said as he entered the room. He was in his shirtsleeves and carried a glass of clear fluid that he sipped. "Hello, Officer Pflam, how is life treating you?"

"Fine, sir. Hope all is well with you." The officer blushed when Preston did not respond.

"Preston," Milton said, "I've got some information for you." He nodded at the detective and then at Dorothea. "Then Officer Pflam and I have to talk with you about a police matter affecting you both."

Spivak took a long drink of coffee, then lit up one of the little cigars he favored. When it was going he exhaled and continued.

Chapter 34

Spivak took a deep breath. Dorothea watched him as the tension rose in her.

He held up a manila envelope and handed it to Preston. "This here envelope came to me at the office inside a bigger one. A cover sheet asked me to find you, Preston, and pass this smaller one along. So here, and I am sorry if it is trouble for you."

She knew Preston was nervous as well. His hand shook a little as he sipped from his glass and set it on the table. He took the letter from Spivak and shook his head.. He tore it open, read the sheets rapidly, and dropped them onto the table. With a sarcastic laugh he looked down at them and picked up his drink. Dorothea watched him closely. Maybe he wouldn't be able to handle whatever was in the letters.

He spoke firmly, answering the silent questions. "One is a formal communication from Inspector Finlay in East Lansing informing me that the state police no longer require my services. There's also a note from Anderson in Grand Rapids telling me that he will no longer pursue legal action against me." Preston drained the glass and placed it on the table. "I am no longer a suspected felon so now I can starve to death as a free man." In a moment he added, "I'll bet it broke Anderson's heart that he didn't send me to jail."

Dorothea didn't know this Anderson. She knew that Preston did not like or trust him. Whatever animosity was between them, she was relieved that Preston did not have to deal with him anymore.

Preston turned away from them to light a cigarette. "There's a check with the letter. It's called my severance pay."

She didn't care about that. Dorothea felt like smiling and clapping her hands. Preston could walk around a free man.

"It is a blow for you, I know." Spivak said. "But for us as well; damn shame to lose a good officer." He held out his hand. " I could put in a word with the chief. Good, experienced officers are hard to find."

After clearing his throat Noah Pflam said, "It would be an honor to work with you, sir."

"Thank you both. I'll think it over. You are good friends. But my health is still not good. For now I'll just stay here and help Dorothea out. Now excuse me. I need to get some rest."

Spivak raised his hand to stop Preston from leaving the room. "Bear with us. One other matter, Officer Pflam?"

Cap in hand Pflam, stepped forward and cleared his throat again. "Dorothea, if you please, a question or two." From his coat pocket he produced a small notebook and pencil. "Did a man name of Mordechai McNeil reside here?"

"Yes, he did. But . . ."

The sergeant reached out and touched her arm. "Dorothea, let's get our questions out of the way. Then, if you have some for us, you can ask them. OK?"

Frustrated she nodded and waited. Preston frowned; the expression aimed at the floor.

"Said Mordechai McNeil resided here until when?"

"Noah, I don't remember. He left one day and did not come back. That was a couple of weeks ago or so. I kept his room for a while then cleaned it out. Needed the rent."

"About five or six weeks." Pflam transcribed the information laboriously. "His clothes and things are still here?"

"Yes; what's going on?"

Noah Pflam looked at his superior.

"OK, better clear this up," Spivak puffed on his cigar for a moment. "We're trying to sort out this fellow's last few days."

"Last few days? Milt, is Mordechai...?" She had suddenly become anxious. Why was she worried?

"Yes, he's dead. As far as we can make out he was murdered. He was hit over the head with a rock several times. Body found a few miles east of here near a grove of trees by a farmer's bridge over the Grand River."

Preston turned away from the group, sat down and relit his cigarette. Dorothea noticed the tremors as he held the match.

"The weather has been cold, not much snow. He was left alongside the dirt road leading to the bridge. A maintenance fellow found him. We identified McNeil from his wallet. Still money in it so robbery wasn't the motive."

Spivak nodded at Noah. "Dorothea, we're going to need to collect McNeil's things. Should take a look at them."

She nodded. "I have everything he left in a chest upstairs in the box room. Come get it any time."

The senior officer stepped forward to put his hand on Preston's shoulder. They faced each other.

"Preston, we got someone who says he saw you and McNeil together. Might have been about the time he went missing."

Preston shrugged and tried to smile. "When I was drinking things weren't clear." He puffed at his cigarette and looked around. "Yeah, I can remember talking with Mordechai, or at least a short fat guy."

"About when?"

"Met him here. Dorothea must have some record of the first time he paid rent. I met him in a bar not long after the shoot-out, Sergeant." Preston flicked ash from his cigarette. "I was drinking a lot. Don't remember much."

"Don't recall what you talked about?" Milton said.

"No details, no. We passed the time of day and he asked me to keep him in mind if I came across anybody who was looking to buy stuff. What? I wasn't listening. Glassware for the house, I think. Maybe silverware. Then he just left."

"About what time?" Spivak's question caused Preston to shake his head.

"Can't even tell you if it was day or night."

Spivak ground out his cigar and donned his hat, nodding to Pflam. "OK, that'll do. Guy by the name of Stumpy Atkens says he saw you and McNeil talking. Stumpy is an old friend of ours. I've arrested him a time or two. Stealing, small stuff mostly. Don't know that I can trust him much."

He waved at his assistant. "Come on, Noah. Maybe we'll go back in the morning and ask Stumpy some more questions."

Spivak turned toward the door and then looked back at them. "Just remembered. Talked at the station with a guy named Moses, Moses McNeil, the dead guy's brother. Pretty torn up about the murder. Says he's going to find the killer." He smiled, "Yeah, it's not likely that an angry amateur can do our work for us. But this Moses seems like a pushy fellow." He turned to the door and then turned back a second time. "Dorothea, you don't have to answer this Moses fellow's questions at all. Let me know if he gets obnoxious."

"Thanks, Milton, I appreciate that."

Coming back from letting the police officers out Dorothea found Preston still seated at the dining table. She stopped, thinking he'd said something to her but found he was muttering to himself.

She'd turn on the fire under the pot of cabbage soup she had prepared for supper, then came back to check on him.

❧   ❧   ❧

"Preston, come on. I'll help you upstairs. You need to rest." Returning to the room, Dorothea found Preston's head slumped as his hand beat steadily on the wooden table. He seemed half asleep or in a muted version of one of those rages he had had in the hospital. The gin he had consumed had not relaxed him this time.

She felt the weight of the conversation she had to have with Preston but first she had to get him to bed and then feed her roomers. Though it was a Sunday, November 10, 1940, and usually she did not fix a supper things had changed when she thought the cabbage might spoil.

The warm soup would be a treat for her guests. They'd

appreciate the care.

❧ ❧ ❧

She had prepared the meal and set out sliced bread. Her roomers would see the note she'd left when they came in. Now she was tired.

Lights turned off and doors locked, Dorothea slowly climbed the stairs a second time to her room. When she entered her room and turned on the overhead light she was surprised for a moment. She'd forgotten that she had put Preston to nap in her bed. He was still sleeping so she snapped off the light and undressed in the dark.

Mutterings and restless tossing under the covers informed her that he'd been roused. At first he seemed to be apologizing to someone, but his voice grew louder and sharper until he rose up in bed, beating the mattress. "You will not." His shout became a refrain as he struck the bed again and again.

"Preston, wake up." She shook him. Finally his eyes opened and she could see the fear.

"A drink," he said.

"No. we have to talk first."

He sat up and struck the bed. "A drink. I need a drink."

"All right, relax. I'll get you a precious drink."

In the cabinet above the sink she had set away a small bottle of scotch. Someone had given it to her and she had put it away since she did not care for the taste.

She got it down and twisted off the cap. When she got a

glass from the shelf he halted her.

"No, no glass. Just give me the bottle." He held out his right hand to show her how badly it was shaking. She handed him the bottle. The whiskey bubbled and sloshed as he took a long drink.

"Ah," he said and shook his head. He threw back the covers and rose to put on his trousers. She sat in the chair while he sat on the bedside. A match flared as he lit a cigarette. "What do you want to talk about?" A smile made his gaunt face seem almost normal.

"Preston, you know something about Mordechai's murder." He was silent. "I know you well enough to know when you are hiding something. We must be honest with each other. It is all that we have now. Tell me."

Chapter 35

Preston turned suddenly toward Dorothea. She was shocked by the despair on his face. The scar on his left jaw was pale in contrast to the flush suffusing his face She stood still as though she half-expected her lover to strike out at her.

"Honest?" Preston's utterance hung in the air of the dark bedroom like a threat. He said it again. "Honesty?"

Dorothea looked away and then back at him. She said, "Yes, we must be honest with each other." Did she mean it? Could she finally be open and honest with him? What would he think, or do?

He took another drink, choked and wiped his mouth. "Well, then, here goes. Two days after the shoot-out with the car thieves I was drinking in a dive. Suddenly this creepy little guy, Mordechai, was asking me questions." He took another quick drink. "You know, he could sound like a preacher asking for an offering or a dentist telling you it wasn't going to hurt. Smooth and convincing, he was." He shook his head emphatically. "He told me some stuff, asked me to do some things I couldn't do."

Dorothea nodded and was silent.

"I think he might have said something about getting more liquor. I still had the Ford. Must have blanked out. Came to. I was behind the wheel, have no idea how I drove. Next I knew we were out in the country and it was colder than hell." Preston screwed the cap on the bottle and put it on the table. He looked down at the floor, lips compressed as if he were done speaking.

"Preston, it was cold, and what happened?" she said. It was time to get all of their secrets out. Dorothea was ready.

"Oh, yeah, honest. You want it all. Honest. When I came to I was standing over him. Had a rock in my hand. He was on the ground, blood all over his head and on the snow." He took a deep breath and tried to unscrew the cap but he must have put it on crookedly since it wouldn't turn. "Damn thing." Tears glittered in his bloodshot eyes.

"I must have hit him. I was the only one around. Threw the rock as far as I could. Dragged him by the feet behind a stump. Looked at him for a while then got in the Ford and drove to a bar somewhere." With a grunt he tore the cap loose and drank the bottle empty.

"You were sure he was dead?"

"People who aren't breathing are usually dead."

"OK, the police don't seem to have much evidence. Maybe Mordechai had other enemies."

"Stumpy, the bartender, saw us together.

"Yes, well tell me the rest."

"What?"

"Why did you go with him? Why did you hit him?"

He coughed and then lit a cigarette. The match, still lit, fell onto the tabletop. He wet his finger and ground it out. "That sneaky little guy wanted me to – you know – help him trap you."

"What? Trap me?" She shivered. What had the sneaky

little man known?

"Remember what you said, Dorothea? About honesty? Well, it's soon going to be your turn."

Preston went on with his story. "In the bar Mordechai told me he suspected you had killed some of the roomers, killed them for their pensions. He wanted me to find some letters, old checks, anything that would show you were still getting their money. He wanted me to sneak around and look through your stuff to see if I could find out how you killed them. Maybe see if I could find out – you know – where you buried them." Preston puffed on the cigarette and exhaled. He looked around the room furtively. "Are they around here?"

Dorothea wrung her hands as a tremor ran up her spine. "Preston, stop it. You felt you had to protect me. Thank you for that, Preston." She shivered again. "You must have suspected me of, of killing roomers."

"Yeah, suspected," he said. "When I had just moved in I got the mail. Remember? You were irritated with me. There was a letter, official looking, for Max, Max Vollman?"

"Volstad."

'Yes, that's the name. McNeil was looking for him, or rather the person still cashing his retirement checks."

Dorothea slumped in her chair. "Yes, I gave Max a shot, of insecticide, nicotine. He died here in this room."

Preston lowered his head into his hands and said, "Here we are. Both of us are killers. Murderers. The type of people I used to chase." The cigarette butt touched his hair. In the silence the crackling of his hair could be heard. A sharp stink of burning hair filled the air.

"Preston."

"Yes, yes, I know." He straightened up and stubbed out the butt. "Now it's all on the table. Both murderers. I did it out of love, to protect you. You did it out of – what – for money?"

She recoiled and shook her head. He was being desperately cruel. His sarcasm dripped from his words as he reached out to her with his right hand saying, "Gee, I'm sorry. Did I not understand correctly? You're not still receiving their money?"

Dorothea struck his hand away. Did he not know her at all? Had she been mistaken about Preston?

"I do get money from some of my guests who died here. But nothing I've done was done through greed. How do you think I keep this rooming house going? Preston, you of all people, should know I am not a greedy person."

She took a breath and went on.

"Can't you understand? Are you so hard, calloused, that you don't recognize love outside a bedroom? Those people were alone, in pain. There was no money for doctors, nor for fancy care. Somebody had to nurse them. I did. I cared."

"You killed them."

"Yes, I eased their dying.."

"How do you know that?"

"Certainly not as much pain as a bullet or a rock."

"An attack, huh? Are we to compare our crimes?"

"Preston, aren't we doing just that?"

He wrenched the cap from the bottle, remembered it was empty and threw it down. "You're getting me all mixed up, dammit."

"Sorry, I don't mean to. We're being honest with each other. Lovers are supposed to do that. We are both murderers, Preston."

"Don't say that."

"You do your . . . deed with a badge. I guess I do mine, how? For love? I just do it. You did it for me? Mordechai McNeil wasn't a criminal."

He struggled to stand up but sat down on the bed. "My head is spinning. I need to get out of here. Get a drink."

Dorothea rose and went to him. Easing him back onto the bed she uttered soothing sounds as one might do to a sick child. "You rest some now, Preston."

"Will you stay with me?"

"Yes, I believe I'll lay down beside you. We both could use a nap."

"I won't be able to sleep."

"OK, then just close your eyes. We'll listen to each other's breathing."

In a few moments they were breathing deeply in unison.

"Preston." Dorothea gently shook him. "Preston, wake up. I've brought something to eat." The tray rested on the bed while she helped him sit up. The vegetable soup was warm and there was buttered bread with coffee.

"Stop shaking your head, Preston. You'll spill the soup. Are you all right?" He shook his head from side to side as if he was trying to clear it. Eyes dull, unfocused, he looked around. "I was in church, heard the organ. Then I was in the confessional. Told the priest about shooting those car thieves. Told him about Pen and Teddy. He was looking at me the whole time. Kind eyes. I know he was going to grant me – what do you call it? Forgiveness."

She shook her head and handed him a bowl of soup. "I'm not the one to ask. Never went to church."

He held the soup bowl in his hand and drank the broth. Dorothea sat in the chair and ate with her spoon. Her slice of bread tasted good dipped in the soup.

"I dreamed of a priest, Father Armand. He was my priest when I was a kid," he said as he finished the meal and set the bowl on the tray.

"He told me to go to a priest and get. . . I can't think of the word." Resting his head on the pillow, he closed his eyes and frowned.

She collected the dishes.

Preston sat up, "Absolution. That's what a priest can give me for my sins. You know, Dorothea, murder is a mortal sin. You could go to hell."

She concentrated on the tray. The dishes clattered and threatened to slide off as she left the room and stepped down on the stairs. Preston was talking like a crazy person. It had her all confused.

In the kitchen she made sure the lights were off. Phil and Tom would come in drunk, as usual but they weren't noisy. Beryl and Minnie would be arriving soon. They made little noise but their giggling was sometimes irritating. Franklin Kelly had had a bit of the soup and made his way slowly up the stairs. Tomorrow she would make a point of checking on him. He was so pale and hadn't felt well for several days now.

The slow climb back up the stairs gave her time to reflect. She could recall the faces of Clement, Max and Alma. Max's visage was twisted and pale. His pain was almost too much for him to bear. But he didn't hurt anymore. She had helped him. Go to hell for helping that poor man? Yes, she nodded emphatically. If she had to.

The money had helped keep Alma until the voices grew too loud, too demanding. Dorothea didn't want to think what fate awaited Alma in an asylum. Asylum, indeed! No, she wasn't afraid of hell. Maybe Preston's mind was clearer; when he was more rested he would understand. If he still wanted to they might talk to a priest.

Chapter 36

After a dog barking on the beach woke her, Dorothea could not get back to sleep. The night had been a struggle for her. Preston tossed and muttered a lot. She heard the two young roomers returning from the bars. Why do drunks believe they can sing? Earlier she'd heard Beryl and Minnie giggling on the stairs as they came up to their rooms.

She sat up on the squeaking mattress. Her back hurt and her eyes felt tender and grainy. She dressed and went down to the kitchen. It was Monday, the beginning of the week. It would do the roomers good to have a hot breakfast. For some reason this morning she couldn't remember the routine. What did she fix?

Franklin Kelly, her newest guest wasn't sixty yet, she bet. He couldn't walk very far nor breathe well. She hoped he came down for breakfast. Lately he had been looking as if he were getting weaker. If he didn't, she must remember to see him, to check on him.

In the kitchen she got the coffee perking. The task was done from habit; she scarcely realized what she was doing. She put the empty pot that had held yesterday's cabbage soup in the sink and filled it with water. Later she'd give it a good scrub.

Dorothea, she scolded silently, what are you going to get

these poor people for their breakfast? In the small room she used as a pantry there were shelves stacked with cans of fruits and vegetables she'd bought on sale. She found some family-size boxes of Kellogg's Corn Flakes she'd forgotten about. They'd cost five cents a box and this morning she could get the milkman to drop off an extra bottle of milk.

She preferred to give the boarders a hot breakfast and this was winter. But she rubbed her eyes and got out the breakfast cereal. She'd cut a corner this once.

This Monday morning, meals followed the typical pattern and were subdued affairs with little conversation or loud talk. Tom and Phil quietly nursed hangovers while the others were always quiet. No one complained about the breakfast and Franklin Kelly did not show up.

With the dishes in soapy water, Dorothea took a break and carried a glass of milk up to Preston. When she entered the room she saw his eyes were open.

"Morning," she said.

He turned his head on the pillow to look at her, "Dorothea, we are sinful. Doomed. Do you know that?" His eyes were intense, fearful.

"Sure do. For a long time."

"We need a priest to take away our sins." He rose on an elbow. "We're going to hell, for sure."

"Yes, dear, I know. Sit up and drink this."

He did as he was told, making faces as he finished the fluid. "Tastes like chalk. He fell back on the pillow and glanced out the window. "What's the weather like?"

Dorothea went to the window. "Sky is mostly clear, not many clouds. The lake is peaceful." For a moment she felt like saying that the heavens were not on fire. She dismissed the words. "Seems like a mild day. Just a few whitecaps. She stepped beside the bed. "Let's do the dishes together. We'll take our time, no hurry. Then we'll take a walk. Okay? Like we used to. We'll walk to the jetty."

Preston sat up and swung his legs to the floor; as he pulled on his trousers he smiled and nodded. The thirst wasn't real strong yet, but he'd need a drink of liquor pretty soon. There ought to be a drink somewhere in the room. He wouldn't ask; it might upset Dorothea.

While Preston slowly got ready. Dorothea hurried down the stairs and started cleaning up the kitchen. While Preston dressed she'd get a head start on supper. She rolled out the meatballs deftly and placed them in the hot oil she'd poured in an iron skillet. She'd boil the spaghetti just before supper. It wouldn't take long.

Preston seemed in a good mood when he came down and started in on the dishes. He looked out the kitchen window at the thermometer mounted there. "It's already in the 30s, Dorothea. Maybe it'll get up into the 50s today."

"Oh, won't that be nice. I can hardly wait to get outdoors."

When the meatballs had been simmering in the oil long enough she added some tomatoes and garlic sliding the skillet to the back of the stove. There they would stay warm but not overcook. Preston was focused on washing the breakfast dishes and did not hear Dorothea behind him. He jumped and made a startled noise when she kissed his neck. When he turned she kissed his lips quickly.

"Preston, I'm going upstairs to look in on Franklin. Want to make sure he's doing all right before we go. The others are out."

He nodded and muttered something before he resumed his work. For a moment Dorothea watched him but then she decided not to say anything. There had been booze on his breath but there was no need to pester the poor man.

≈ ≈ ≈

"Come in." Franklin said.

"Hope I didn't wake you."

He smiled up at her from his position on his back in bed. "Sorry I didn't get up, Dorothea. My leg is a mite tender this morning." He took a deep breath. "Having trouble with the lungs too."

"You look pale. You haven't had much of an appetite. Can I do anything to make you more comfortable?"

"Bless you, Dorothea. When I can't breath I don't have a yen for food. It's not your cooking, no sir."

The little man lay still and panting. She sensed that he needed help so she waited patiently.

"It's a cross," Franklin said. "A real cross when I can't get enough air."

"Poor man, I imagine it is. Maybe another pillow?"

"That would be nice."

When she had propped him up on a second pillow, she asked, "Franklin, how about a couple of those white pills I gave you that other time, aspirins?"

"Oh, I think they might ease things. And, Dorothea?" She stopped at the door. "Maybe some of that Vicks stuff. That salve for my chest?" She nodded and left to get the medicine.

❧   ❧   ❧

"Maybe tomorrow we can find a church, get a priest to take away our sins." Preston spoke above the freshening breeze. They had stopped to rest for a moment at the light jetty. Dorothea stopped to light a cigarette and tried not to be irritated with him. Since they left the house he had talked about priests, confession and removing sins. Why couldn't he enjoy the exhilarating day? The waves splashed her and she couldn't light her cigarette so she threw it away

"We'll try if you want." Dorothea said. She inhaled deeply and looked at the waves hitting the beach. The wind had picked up a bit and the sky was changing from china white to gray. Perhaps there'd be a few snowflakes but she wanted to walk out on the pier, to get closer to the water.

The jetty was formed by large chunks of concrete held in place by a heavy steel enclosure. Dorothea laughed and laughed again at the thrill of the Lake as the freshening wind whipped the sounds from her lips. She climbed onto the uneven surface of the wharf and then helped Preston to clamber up.

She held his head close so that she could speak into his ear. "Let's go out to the end of the jetty."

"The waves are getting stronger. We'll get wet." He said.

"That won't matter, Preston. Come on with me. We'll be

surrounded by the water."

"I'll follow you, Dorothea," he yelled into the wind and held her hand more tightly.

"Just come with me, dear. It will be all right."

承 承 承

SPECIAL

Newspaper Wire Service

A nation celebrating Armistice Day this Monday November 11, 1940 was shocked by the eruption of Lake Michigan into the worst storm on record.

A rare freshwater cyclone struck the east coast of the lower peninsula of the state at about 2:30 P.M. with unimaginable force. The temperature plummeted in less than an hour from 50 degrees to freezing. Rain drenched the unfortunate towns and soon turned into snow that soon accumulated in impassable drifts.

Sailors trapped on their vessels were doomed. The railroad car ferry *City of Flint* was beached near Lake Harbor. *The Indian*, and the *Richard H.*, fishing boats sank with the loss of eight crewmen. Three freighters—

SS Anna C. Minch, SS William B. Dovack, and SS Novador sank – Taking their crews of 66 souls to a watery grave.

Ashore the situation was no less deadly. Duck hunters, enjoying the mild morning weather, were trapped in their blinds by frigid weather and rising waters. Many were washed into the raging Lake waters. Buildings were destroyed, power lines blown down starting many fires.

So far 154 bodies of unfortunates have been found. Desperate rescue efforts continue, but little hope remains.

A shocked nation mourns its loss.

About the Author

Dave Bachelor has been a teacher his entire working life. The joy of teaching is searching alongside the students (searchers). Addicted to this teaching "high" Bachelor took up writing fiction swhen he retired. As a story unfolds the he is often as surprised as his readers by its developments. Everyone gets in on the thrill. So this retired history high school teacher, professor of sociology of education and educational research, continues to write novels. His latest is *Dorothea and Preston: a story of love.*

www.ingramcontent.com/pod-product-compliance
Lightning Source LLC
Chambersburg PA
CBHW031104260626
47172CB00001B/208